Enid Blyton

BOTTOM OF THE CLASS!

and other stories

Illustrated by
Paul Crompton

D1645293

World International Publishing Limited
Manchester

Published in Great Britain by World International
Publishing Limited,
An Egmont Company, Egmont House, PO Box 111,
Great Ducie Street,
Manchester M60 3BL.
Printed in Italy.

British Library Cataloguing in Publication Data
Blyton, Enid 1897–1968
Bottom of the class and other stories.
I. Title II. Series
823.912 [J]

ISBN 0–7498–0316–9

Cover illustration by Robin Lawrie

Contents

Bottom of the class!	7
Sammy and the spider	16
The robber who wasn't there	24
A pair of pickles	33
When the moon was blue	41
The well-mannered scarecrow	66
Nobody came to tea	73
Slowcoach Sammy	78
The tail of Bup the bunny	86
The tale of Tinker the pup	95
Sneezing powder	103
Trundle goes out to tea	111
It grew and it grew	122
Tale of a teddy and a mouse	130
In the King's shoes	145
The goblin and the dragon	157
Goldie and the water sprite	167
Oh, what a pity!	177

Enid Blyton

Enid Blyton was born in London in 1897. Her childhood was spent in Beckenham, Kent, and as a child she began to write poems, stories and plays. She trained to be a teacher but she devoted her whole life to being a children's author. Her first book was a collection of poems for children, published in 1922. In 1926 she began to write a weekly magazine for children called *Sunny Stories*, and it was here that many of her most popular stories and characters first appeared. The magazine was immensely popular and in 1953 it became *The Enid Blyton Magazine*.

She wrote more than 600 books for children and many of her most popular series are still published all over the world. Her books have been translated into over 30 languages. Enid Blyton died in 1968.

Bottom of the class!

Somebody always has to be at the bottom of every class. "But," said Miss Brown, "it needn't always be the *same* person, Bobby!"

You see, Bobby was *always* at the bottom. He was very sorry about it, but he couldn't help it. He had been ill for two years of his school life, and that meant that he was far behind everyone else.

He wasn't very good at handiwork, either, because he was left-handed, and that seemed to make him awkward with the raffia or the cane that the class used to make baskets.

He was bad at games because he wasn't strong and couldn't run fast.

His mother was often very sorry for the little boy, because he never once grumbled or complained, and yet she knew he must be unhappy about it.

There was one thing that Bobby was very, very fond of, and that was gardening. He might not be able to run fast, but you should see him weeding! And the flowers didn't mind whether he was left-handed or right-handed, because he always knew when to water them, when to weed, and when to tie them up so that the wind couldn't blow them down.

"You know, Daddy," his mother said to his father, "Bobby isn't much good at anything except gardening. So we must help him all we can with that. When people aren't much good at anything, and can't help it, it's very important to find *something* they like and can do really well. And gardening is what Bobby likes best of all."

So his parents gave Bobby a very big piece of the garden. They bought him a spade and fork, watering-can, trowels, dibbers, raffia for tying, and a fine wheelbarrow. He was delighted.

"Oh, *thank* you!" he said. "Now I'll really be able to grow marvellous flowers. And, Mummy, do you know what I shall do? I shall grow enough flowers for you to have them all over the house, and enough to take to Miss Brown twice a week to keep our classroom beautiful. Then she'll know that even if I'm at the bottom of the class and stay there, I can at least *do something*!"

He kept his word. He worked hard in his garden each day. He dug, he weeded, he sowed, he watered. He thinned out his seedlings, he put soot down to keep away slugs, he tied up his tall plants so that the wind should not break them.

And all the term his mother had her house full of flowers from Bobby's garden, and, really, you should have seen Bobby's classroom! There were roses on the mantelpiece, lupins on the window-sill, pinks on the bookcase smelling as sweet as sugar. Miss Brown said they never had so many lovely flowers, and all the children were grateful to Bobby and his gardening.

The summer term went on. There was to be a concert and a handiwork show at the end. Bobby wasn't in anything at the concert, except in the opening song, because he simply couldn't remember the words in any play or recitation for more than a day. He couldn't even sing in tune, so Miss Brown told him not to sing too loudly in the opening song, in case he put the others off.

Bobby was the only child who had nothing on show in the handiwork display. He had been trying to make a basket, like the others, but it was so bad that Miss Brown said she was sorry, but she couldn't possibly show it.

The lady at the big house was to come to hear the concert and open the show.

But on the day before the concert she fell ill and couldn't come. The children were sorry, because they liked her. But she sent rather an exciting message. "I have asked a friend of mine to come instead," she said. "She is a duchess, so I hope you will welcome her nicely and thank her properly for coming."

"A duchess!" said the children. "Goodness, Miss Brown – we'll all have to be extra smart, and won't we have to present her with a bouquet – a really beautiful bunch of flowers?"

"Yes, we shall," said Miss Brown. "I must order some at once. Now – who shall give the flowers to her?"

The top girl of the class felt certain *she* would be chosen. The boy who happened to be games captain just then hoped *he* would be. Suzette, the smartest girl in the class, remembered her beautiful new silk frock, and thought *she* ought to be the one to curtsey and present the flowers.

11

But suddenly little Mary spoke up. "Miss Brown, *I* think Bobby ought to present the bouquet! Look at all the lovely flowers he's grown for us this term. He ought to have some reward – and he's not doing anything special in the concert, and he's got nothing in the handiwork show. I do think he ought to present the flowers."

There was a moment's silence and then all the children – yes, even the top girl, the games captain and Suzette – shouted out loudly: "Yes! *yes*! That's fair. Let Bobby do it! Let Bobby give the flowers!"

What an honour for Bobby. He sat blushing in his seat, his eyes shining. What would his mother say when she saw him going up to the Duchess and bowing and presenting the bouquet? Bobby was as glad for his mother as he was for himself.

It was all settled – except that Bobby insisted that he should bring the bouquet from his own garden. "I've got the loveliest carnations and roses this week you ever saw," he said. "Better than in any of the shops. Real beauties – and I'd love to give them to the Duchess."

So Bobby picked his carnations and roses, made them into a magnificent bouquet, and took them to school the next afternoon. All the mothers were there, and some of the fathers. It was a great day for the school and the parents.

The pretty Duchess drove up in a lovely black car. The children cheered. She smiled and went up on to the little platform to speak to the children.

And then, very proudly, Bobby went up on to the platform, too, carrying the flowers he had grown himself. He looked neat and tidy, his hair was well brushed, his shoes shone, and his nails were clean. Miss Brown was proud of him.

Bobby bowed and presented the bouquet to the Duchess. His mother almost cried for joy. The Duchess took

the flowers and exclaimed over them:
"How beautiful! I have never, never
had such a wonderful bouquet before!

Oh, thank you. What *glorious* roses and carnations!"

Little Mary couldn't stop herself from calling out: "Bobby grew them himself! He picked them out of his own garden for you!"

"Good gracious! What a clever boy you must be!" said the Duchess. "How proud your school must be of you!"

Bobby was as red as a beetroot. He almost burst for joy. He was at the bottom of the form and always had been – and here he was being told he was clever by the Duchess herself – and he *knew* the school was proud of him!

So they were. They were proud of him and they liked him. As for his mother, how she beamed when all the other mothers crowded round her afterwards, and praised her Bobby!

Bobby's grown up now. He is the head of a very fine flower-growing firm. He takes all the prizes there are. It's surprising what you can do, even if you *are* at the bottom of the class!

Sammy and the spider

There was once a boy called Sammy who was afraid of spiders. If he saw one running across the room he would squeal in fright.

"Don't be silly, Sammy," said his mother. "A spider can't hurt you!"

"I don't like all its legs," said Sammy.

"But my dear child, a caterpillar has plenty of legs, and you pick those up!" said his mother.

"I know," said Sammy. "But I just don't like spiders. I'm going to stamp on that one and kill it."

"Sammy, don't do that," said his mother. "Why should you take away a spider's life just because you don't happen to like it? I'd be very sorry if somebody was to stamp on *you* just because they didn't like you."

"Well – it does seem unkind," said Sammy. "But let me shoo it out of the room, Mummy!"

His mother got a shovel, let the spider run on to it, and then she dropped it out of the window.

"You must be kind to things even if you don't like them," she said. "Don't turn yourself into somebody cruel and unthinking, when you see something you are afraid of. Don't be afraid of it, and you won't feel unkind!"

"That's difficult," said Sammy. But because he knew that his mother was wise and kind herself, he tried to remember what she said.

Now one day a most enormous spider came into Sammy's bedroom. It really was a *giant*. It had eight legs, of course, and it ran like clockwork on them. Sammy stared at the spider, feeling really afraid.

"I must kill it!" he said to himself.

Then he thought again. "But after all, it can't *help* being a spider. Perhaps it would rather not be. But it has to be because it came out of a spider's egg. I shan't kill it. Mummy's right – it's bad to hurt something just because you don't happen to like it. But what shall I do with it?"

Sammy could not bear to touch the big spider. So he got his cricket bat and let the spider run on to it. Then he took the bat to the window and shook it smartly. The spider dropped off it on to the hedge below. Sammy couldn't see where it went.

"Well, that's good," he thought. "I hope it won't come back again. I'm glad I didn't stamp on it."

No more spiders came into Sammy's room that autumn, and he didn't think any more about them. Then his birthday came, and he was tremendously excited.

He had a new bicycle, with a bell, a basket, and a saddle-bag. That was simply marvellous. He had a football, and he had a toy aeroplane that really flew well.

His uncle sent him a postal order. "Buy yourself a new paintbox," he wrote in a letter. "I know you want one."

"That's just what I *do* want!" said Sammy joyfully. "Mummy, what do I do with this paper money?"

"You take it down to the post office, and they will give you money for it," said Mummy. "Take it tomorrow, because it's Saturday and you will have lots of time."

So Sammy left the paper money in his bedroom till the next day, and a dreadful thing happened! The wind came in at the window, took hold of the paper money and whisked it right away!

Sammy ran to catch it – but the wind took it out of the window at the top, where it was open. Sammy gave a yell. There was his paper money flying away on the wind!

He tore downstairs to find it. He rushed into the garden and looked on the ground everywhere. But the paper money had quite disappeared. It was a great shock for poor Sammy.

"Darling, it's no good looking any more," said Mummy, at last. "It will have blown miles away by now. There is such a tremendous wind today. Never mind. You have lots of lovely presents, and maybe someone will give you a paintbox for Christmas."

All the same Sammy was very, very sad. It was dreadful to lose the money. He had felt so rich – and now he felt so poor.

He went out into the garden to play with his football. He kicked it high into the air, and it landed on top of the privet hedge. Sammy went to get it.

And he saw a most strange and amazing sight. There was a very large web on the hedge, made by a giant of a spider, who was lurking at one end. No flies had been caught in the web – but

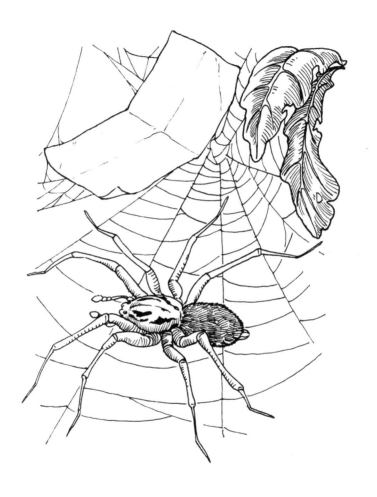

something else had been caught! Yes – you've guessed right! Sammy's paper money had blown right into the sticky web, and there it was, safely held.

Sammy couldn't believe his eyes. He stared and stared. Then he gave such a shout that the spider ran deep into the hedge. Sammy carefully pulled the paper money from the web, and looked to see if he could find the spider.

It came up to the web. It was really a *giant*.

"You're the very same spider I put out of my window weeks ago!" said Sammy. "You are, really. And you've made a marvellous web – and that web caught my paper money when it blew away. So if you like doing a good turn to repay one done to you, spider, you may feel happy! I'm very, very pleased I let you go, and very, very pleased I've got my money back!"

The spider looked at Sammy. Then it ran into the middle of its web.

"I'm not afraid of you any more," said

Sammy. "Not one single bit. You're a friend, not an enemy! You've saved my money. I shall always like spiders after this!"

He ran indoors to tell his mother. She was simply delighted. "Well, one good turn deserves another," she said, "but I'm sure it isn't often that a spider can do a thing like *that*, Sammy!"

Sammy got his paintbox, and now he is going in for every painting competition. I wonder if he will win a prize, don't you?

The robber who wasn't there

It was a lovely spring day, and the sun shone down warmly. The primroses began to open in the garden, and George and Nora went to pick a bunch for the playroom table.

Happy, their dog, went with them. He ran round the garden, smelling here and there, just as happy as his name. He ran to the garden shed and sniffed around.

Suddenly he cocked up his ears and then began to bark madly! How he barked!

"Woof, woof, woof! Woof, woof, woof!"

"Whatever's the matter, Happy?" cried Nora, in surprise. "You'll bark your head off, then what will you do?"

"Woof, woof, woof!" barked Happy, and he scraped at the shed door with his paw.

"He wants to go in," said George. "I wonder why?"

Happy stopped barking and stood listening to something inside the shed, his head well on one side. The children listened too.

There was a noise inside the shed! It was a funny noise – a kind of scrapy, scrambly noise – and then a pot fell over and broke!

The children jumped and looked scared.

"Woof, woof, woof!" barked Happy again, and he scraped at the wooden door as if he would like to break it down.

"There's somebody hiding in there," said Nora.

"Who could it be?" said George, in a frightened whisper.

"A robber!" whispered back Nora. "Oh dear, George, I feel frightened. Let's go and tell Mummy."

They waited for a moment, and then they heard the noise inside the shed again. Another pot fell over, and the children jumped and ran away. Happy stayed behind, barking, and pawing at the door.

"There's one thing – the robber won't escape from the shed whilst Happy is barking outside," panted George, as the two children ran to the house.

"No – so he's a prisoner till we get somebody to catch him!" said Nora.

They rushed into the house and called for their mother. "Mummy! Mummy! Come quickly! Where are you?"

But Mummy was out. So they ran to tell Jane their big sister. "Jane! Jane! There's a robber in the garden shed!" said George. "Will you come and catch him?"

"Good gracious, no!" cried Jane, quite alarmed. "I'm certainly not going robber-catching! I'll tell Cook!"

So Jane, George and Nora ran to the kitchen to tell the cook about the robber in the garden shed. Cook was surprised to see them all running at top speed into her kitchen.

"What's the matter?" she said.

"Oh, Cook, there's a robber in the garden shed!" panted Jane. "Get your rolling pin and come and catch him."

"Indeed, I won't," said Cook at once. "A robber should be caught by the policeman. He'll be by here soon. We'll watch for him and tell him. Fancy that now – a robber in the garden shed!"

"Happy is keeping him prisoner till we get somebody to catch the robber," said Nora, feeling tremendously excited. "Can't you hear him barking like mad?"

They could. "Woof, woof, woof!"

"Here comes the policeman!" said Cook at last, and they saw the big burly policeman walking slowly down their road. George, Nora, Jane, and Cook all flew out to the front gate and called to him.

"Oh, Mr Policeman! We've got a robber here!"

"What did you say?" asked the policeman in great surprise, and he took out his notebook and pencil.

"Oh, there's no time to be writing notes," cried Jane. "There's a robber in the garden shed and the dog's guarding him. He'll be a very fierce robber, and maybe he'll fight you, Mr Policeman. Hadn't you better get someone to help you?"

"Oh no," said the policeman, rather grandly. "I'm quite used to robbers."

So George, Nora, Jane, Cook, and the policeman all went down the garden to the shed, where Happy was still barking.

"Now just listen, everyone!" said George.

So they all listened, and sure enough they could hear the noise in the shed all right – and two more pots fell over with a crash! Even the policeman jumped, and as for Jane, she ran half-way up the garden in fright.

"Now here's a strange thing," said

the policeman, suddenly pointing to the door. "It's locked on the outside, there's the key in the lock, and it's turned! Now how did the robber get in there, and yet lock the door on the outside?"

Everybody stared at the lock, but nobody could think how a robber could lock himself in and yet leave the key outside. It was a mystery.

The policeman unlocked the door and shouted out in a loud, stern voice, "Come out, there! Come out at once!"

Everyone waited to see who would come out – but nobody did! Another plant pot fell over. The policeman grew angry.

"Am I to come in after you? Come out at once!" But still nobody came out. So the policeman bravely stuck his head inside the dark shed and looked around.

"There's nobody here!" he said in the greatest astonishment. "Well – that's odd!"

Everybody looked inside – and sure

enough there was no robber there at all. Happy darted round and round the shed, sniffing happily. Everyone went out again and talked hard.

"Then who made that noise?"

"There *was* somebody there!"

"And it must have been a robber!"

"How could he have got away?"

And suddenly they heard the noise again! They all stared at the door, feeling quite scared.

Then the robber walked out! Yes — he really did! And who do you suppose it was? Why, nobody else but Crawler, the old tortoise, who had been put there asleep in a box for the winter! He had woken up, scrambled out of his box, and crawled round the shed, knocking over pots as he went. Well, well, well!

He walked out into the warm spring sunshine, and blinked his eyes at everyone. Happy danced round him, barking. Everyone went red and looked foolish.

Then George laughed — and Nora

joined in. Jane giggled and Cook roared. The policeman opened his mouth and ha-ha-ha'd too. It was surprising to hear them, and Crawler the tortoise was frightened. He popped his head under his shell!

"The robber who wasn't there!" cried Nora, pointing to the tortoise. "Oh, Crawler, what a fright you gave us!"

A pair of pickles

Billy and Bessie were a pair of pickles. You never knew what mischief they would be up to next!

They dirtied their clothes every day. They lost things. They came in muddy and never thought of wiping their shoes. Well, really, I can't tell you half the things they did, because I would need about ten books to put them in!

Everybody called them "the Pickles". "Where are those Pickles?" Mummy would say at dinner time. "It is time they were home."

"Hello, Pickles!" people would say. Billy and Bessie thought it was fun to be two pickles. They didn't think of the worry they made for their mother.

Now one day a funny little fellow came wandering into our land. He was helper to Mister Grumpy-Wumps, the enchanter of Heyho Wood, and Mister Grumpy-Wumps was in one of his tempers.

He always was on Mondays, because he had cold meat for dinner, and he hated it.

"Cold meat again!" he would shout to his helper. "How dare you!"

"Well, it's Monday," said the helper. "And everyone has cold meat on Monday, sir."

"Well, give me something nice to eat with it!" shouted the enchanter. So sometimes the helper gave him beetroot, sometimes he gave him tomato sauce or celery, and sometimes horseradish and cream.

And then one day Mister Grumpy-Wumps took it into his head to want pickles!

"Pickles!" said the helper in surprise. "I've never heard of them. Can't have pickles, Mister Grumpy-Wumps!"

"How dare you tell me that I can't have something I want!" roared Grumpy-Wumps, and for a moment he looked so fierce that he quite startled the little helper. "Go out and bring me pickles. Don't dare to come back till you've got them!"

"Where do I get them?" asked the helper, putting on his hat.

"How do I know?" said the enchanter. "They may grow on trees. They may be sold in a shop. They may sit on chimney-pots. They may walk about in the fields. Anyway, go and get some."

So that was how the little helper happened to come wandering into our land, looking for pickles. And it so happened that he met Bessie and Billy, who were in mischief as usual, paddling in the muddy pond.

"Hello!" said the little fellow.

"Hello!" said the Pickles.

"I'm looking for something," said the

helper. "Can you help me, I wonder? I'm looking for pickles."

Billy laughed. "*We* are pickles!" he said.

"Don't be silly," said the little man sharply.

"I'm not silly," said Billy. "Anybody will tell you we're pickles. Go and ask that lady over there."

The lady was the wife of the farmer. The little man went over to her and raised his hat politely. "Could you please tell me if those two children are pickles?" he asked.

"They certainly are!" said the farmer's wife, with a smile. "Real pickles!"

"Thank you," said the helper, puzzled. So the children *were* pickles. Well, well, well! He would have to take them to Mister Grumpy-Wumps, that's all.

So he went back to them and took them firmly by the hands. "You must come with me," he said. "My master, Mister Grumpy-Wumps, always has cold meat for his dinner on Mondays, and today is Monday, and he told me to go and get him pickles to eat with his dinner. So I'm afraid you must come."

"We won't! We won't!" cried Bessie. "We're not the kind of pickles you eat! Let us go!"

But the helper wouldn't. No, he made the two Pickles go with him to his own land, and he took them right to the enchanter's castle and led them up to Mister Grumpy-Wumps.

"I've brought you the Pickles," he said.

The enchanter stared at the children in dismay. He was really a very kind-hearted fellow, and he knew he couldn't possibly eat this sort of pickle. Well, well! To think that children were pickles! What a very astonishing thing!

"Please don't think we're pickles to eat," said Billy. "We're not!"

"That lady you pointed out to me said you *were*!" said the helper. "She said you were real pickles."

"Well," said the enchanter, going

rather red, "somehow I don't feel like pickles today. Take the children back, you silly man and when I feel like pickles again, you can fetch them. But today I really don't. I think I'll have beetroot instead."

"How you do change your mind!" grumbled the helper, going to fetch the beetroot. As soon as he was out of the room the children ran through another door and tore home as fast as ever they could. They didn't know how glad Mister Grumpy-Wumps was to see them go! Good gracious! How could anyone eat pickles like that!

When they got home the children sat down quietly in a corner. "I'm going to stop being naughty enough to be called a pickle," whispered Bessie to Billy. "After all, we do upset Mummy when we get so dirty and our clothes so torn. Let's be good for a change."

So now they are really very good, and Mummy can't imagine why. She also doesn't know where one of her jars of home-made pickles has gone to, that the children begged from her. But *I* know! It's hidden inside a hollow tree ready to give to the little helper if ever he comes hunting for pickles again.

"He shan't make a mistake *next* time!" says Billy. What a treat for old Grumpy-Wumps when he tastes *real* pickles!

When the moon was blue

One evening, when Jack and Mary were going to bed, they forgot to clean their teeth. Mummy saw their toothbrushes lying beside their tooth-mugs and called to them.

"You naughty children! You haven't cleaned your teeth!"

"We forgot!" said Jack, and the two ran to get their brushes. "Have you ever forgotten to clean your teeth, Mummy?"

"Oh, I daresay I have," said Mummy.

"How often?" asked Mary.

"Oh, once in a blue moon!" said their Mummy, drawing back the curtains so that the air could come into the room.

"What's a blue moon?" said Jack.

"I really don't know," said Mummy.

"Just an ordinary moon turned blue, I expect. I've never seen one."

"You often say things happen 'once in a blue moon'," said Mary. "But a blue moon never comes."

"Well – it might some day!" laughed Mummy. "You'd better be careful then – for goodness knows what might happen if the moon turned blue!"

The children got into bed. Mummy kissed them and said goodnight. Then she turned out the light and went downstairs.

"It's very light out of doors tonight," said Mary. "The moon must be up."

"Daddy said it would be a full moon tonight," said Jack. "Oh, Mary – wouldn't it be exciting if it was blue!"

"Yes, but it won't be," said Mary sleepily. "Things like that never seem to happen. Think how often we've tried to see fairies and never have – and how often we've wished wishes and they haven't come true – and tried to work spells and they won't work. I don't

42

believe in those things any more!"

"I still do," said Jack, "because once one of my wishes really did come true."

"Well, it must have been an accident, then," said Mary, yawning. "Goodnight, Jack. I'm going to sleep."

Both children fell fast asleep in a minute or two. They slept soundly, and didn't hear the wardrobe creaking loudly. They didn't hear the cat mewing outside either.

But when twelve o'clock struck, they did hear something. At least Jack did. He heard an owl hooting outside the window, and he opened his eyes.

"Wit-wit!" said the owl, "woo-wit-wit!"

Jack sat up and wondered what time it was. He looked at the window. A good deal of light came in from outside, for the moon was full. It had gone behind a cloud for a moment, quite a small one, for Jack could see the moon skimming along behind it. He watched it, waiting for it to come out again.

And when it did he gasped and stared

and rubbed his eyes – for what do you suppose? Why, the big round moon was as blue as forget-me-nots! There it shone in the sky, looking very peculiar indeed.

"There's a blue moon!" cried Jack. "Mary, Mary, wake up! There's a blue moon!"

Mary woke up with a jump and sat up. She stared at the moon in the greatest surprise.

"So there is!" she said. "Oh, Jack – do you suppose anything extraordinary will happen? Oh, do let's go to the window and see if we can spy any fairies or pixies about. Mummy said we might see them once in a blue moon!"

They ran to the window – and looked down their moonlit garden. But not a fairy or pixie could they see.

"Let's wish a few wishes!" said Jack, gazing up at the bright blue moon. "They might come true now the moon is blue."

"Yes, let's," said Mary. "I wish we could see a fairy or a gnome or something!"

"And I wish we could, too!" said Jack.

And immediately they did! A gnome, very small and bent, ran out from under the lilac bush in the middle of the garden, and went to the little round pool. In the middle of this was a little statue of a bunny, sitting on a big flat stone.

The gnome jumped over the water and landed beside the bunny. At once the stone rabbit took his hand and stood up. The gnome began to pull at the flat stone on which the bunny had been sitting – and before the children's very eyes, he suddenly disappeared! The stone bunny sat down again and made no movement.

"Did you see that, Mary?" cried Jack. "Come on, quickly! We'll see where he disappeared to. Put on your dressing-gown and I'll put on mine."

They threw on their dressing-gowns

and ran quietly down the stairs. Out they went into the garden and ran to the pond. With a leap Jack was over the water and standing beside the stone bunny in the middle of the pond. To his enormous surprise, the small rabbit at once put a cold paw into his hand and got up. Jack turned to the flat stone – and saw an iron ring on it, and the stone came up. Under it lay a steep stone stairway!

"Come on, Mary!" cried Jack. "Here's an adventure for us! We've always wanted one!"

Mary jumped over the water beside Jack, and peered down the steps. The stone rabbit put its other paw into her hand, and looked beseechingly at her.

"This little rabbit's alive, although it's just a statue!" said Mary, in surprise. "Can you speak, Bunny?"

"Yes," said the rabbit. "I can speak once in a blue moon – and the moon is blue tonight!"

"Are you really a statue or are you alive?" asked Jack.

"I was once the first rabbit in the carriage of the Princess Philomela of Heylo Land," said the bunny. "But one night the wicked gnome Twisty lay in wait for her carriage – and put a log in our path. So over I went and all the other three rabbits, and the Princess fell out of the carriage. The gnome picked her up and carried her off – and turned me and the other rabbits into stone. He sold us for the middles of ponds and there we stayed!"

"Goodness me!" said Jack, in the greatest surprise. "Whoever would have thought of such a thing? Where is the Princess now?"

"I don't know," said the rabbit, mournfully. "She's still a prisoner somewhere, I expect. The gnome has a secret way to Fairyland down that stairway. He may have gone to the Princess now."

"Well, let's go after him then!" said

Jack. "We may see where he keeps the Princess, and perhaps be able to rescue her! Will you come with us, Bunny?"

"Yes, but I'm made of stone, and I would make so much noise!" said the rabbit.

"I'll wish you alive again!" said Jack. "It seems as if wishes come true once in a blue moon!"

"Yes, wish!" said Mary. So Jack wished hard.

"I wish this stone bunny may come alive!" he said – and immediately his wish came true! The little rabbit grew soft and warm and furry – and whiskers grew out of his cheeks. The stone bunny had had no whiskers at all.

"I'm alive. I'm alive!" he cried, frisking round and nearly falling into the pond.

"Mind! You'll fall in the water!" said Mary, clutching hold of the excited bunny. "Come along. We'll go down the steps now."

So down the steps they all went, Jack first, then the bunny, then Mary. It was dark when they got to the bottom, but a lamp hung a little way farther on, and showed them a narrow passage. They went along, most excited.

After a while they came to a turnstile, and they pushed against it. It wouldn't turn round, and Jack thought they had better climb over it. But before he could do so, a small brownie popped his head out of a window in the wall of the passage and said: "Penny each, please."

"We haven't any pennies," said Jack. "We are in our dressing-gowns, and we don't keep pennies there. Please let us through. Has the Twisty Gnome gone this way?"

"Yes, he has," said the brownie, nodding his head. "He often goes this way. No one else goes, except myself – and I only go once in a blue moon!"

"Well, it's a blue moon tonight!" said Jack. "We've seen it!"

"What!" cried the brownie, his face full of excitement. "The moon is blue! My stars, I must go and look!"

He squeezed himself through the window in the wall of the passage, pushed past Jack, Mary and the rabbit and disappeared up the tunnel.

"Come on, let's climb over, now he's gone!" said Mary. So they all climbed over the turnstile, and went on down the tunnel again. But it didn't go very far this time. It opened out into a cave through which a dark, swift river ran. A little pixie sat by the side of some boats, half-asleep.

"Wake up!" cried Jack, running to him. "Has the Twisty Gnome gone this way?"

"Yes, down the river," said the pixie, in surprise. "But he said I was to let no one else but him have my boats today."

"Oh, well, it can't matter once in a blue moon!" said Jack, getting into one.

"What, is the moon blue?" cried the pixie, in delight. "Oh, have my boats then, have them all if you want to! I'm going up to see the moon, the moon, the moon!"

He sat down on a big toadstool growing nearby, and, to the children's great amazement, shot upwards at a great speed.

"Well, I suppose he's gone to see the moon, like the brownie," said Jack. "Come on, Mary and Bunny! We mustn't let the Twisty Gnome get too far ahead!"

They set off in the boat. Jack steered, but there was no need for oars, for the river was very strong and took them along itself. In a few minutes it came out into the open air, and there, hanging in the sky, was the moon, still as blue as forget-me-nots!

As the boat went along, Jack caught sight of a large notice on one of the banks. He looked at it. To his great surprise, it had one word on it:

JUMP!

"Jump," said Jack, puzzled; "why jump?"

"Oh, look!" cried Mary, pointing

ahead. "There is a waterfall or something coming. Jack, if we don't jump, we shall go over the falls. Oh, I'm frightened!"

"Come with me," the bunny said. He took the strings from Jack and pulled the boat towards the bank. It ran into it with a bump, and at the same time all three jumped out! They landed on the soft grass and rolled over. Just ahead of them the river shot over the falls with a roar. Their boat spun round once and then headed for the waterfall. Over it went, and that was the last they saw of it!

"Goodness! I hope this sort of thing only happens once in a blue moon!" said Jack.

"Oh, it does," said the bunny. "Come on. Do you see that castle over there? I am sure that is where the gnome has gone. It belongs to him. Perhaps he has the Princess Philomela locked up in one of the rooms."

They all set off for the castle. They

soon arrived there, and looked up at it. It was very big, and had hundreds of windows, and a great wooden door.

"I don't think I want to go in that door," said Mary. "It looks as if it might shut behind us and make us prisoners in the castle, too. Isn't there another way of getting in?"

"We'll spy round and see," said Jack. So they walked all round the castle – and right at the back they discovered a very small door, painted a bright yellow. Jack pushed it – and it came open!

He and the others peeped inside. It led into a great yard. They all went inside and looked round. The kitchen door stood open and a smell of cakes being baked came out.

"Come on," said Jack. "We may be able to sneak inside."

He crept up to the kitchen door – and at that moment a large gnome-woman came to it to shake a duster. She stared at the three in surprise. They didn't know what to say.

"Oh," she said at last. "I suppose you have come with a message for the Twisty Gnome. You are not the washing, are you? Or the baker?"

"Oh, no!" said Jack. "May we go inside and see the gnome?"

Mary was horrified to hear Jack ask this, for she certainly didn't want to see the horrid Twisty Gnome, in case they were all taken prisoners. The gnome servant nodded her head.

"He's just upstairs with the Princess," she said. "But he won't be long. Come and wait in the hall."

She took them inside and led them to a great hall. They sat down on a bench and she disappeared back into the kitchen.

"Did you hear that?" said Jack. "She said the Twisty Gnome was upstairs with the Princess! So she *is* here! We'll rescue her! Come on – we must hide before the gnome comes back. I don't want to see him, of course – that was only an excuse to get inside!"

Jack, Mary and the rabbit looked round to see where they could hide. There was a long curtain hanging at the foot of the stairs, and the three crept behind it. They hadn't been there more than a minute or two when they heard footsteps coming down the stairs. It was the Twisty Gnome.

As he came into the hall, the gnome-woman ran out. "Master," she said, "there are three . . ."

She stopped short and looked round in surprise – for she could not see Mary, Jack or the bunny. "How strange!" she said. "A boy and a girl and a rabbit came to see you. They were here just now!"

"Oh, indeed!" said Twisty, in a hoarse and threatening voice. "They were here, were they? Well, where are they now? I suppose you've let them go into my magic room, and disturb my spells. Grrrrrr! If you have, I'll turn you into a dustbin lid. That's all you're fit for!"

"Oh, Master, I don't think they've gone into your magic room!" cried the servant – but the gnome had disappeared into a little room on the opposite side of the hall. The servant followed – and in a trice Mary, Jack and the rabbit slipped out from the curtain and were running upstairs as fast as they could.

At each landing there was a locked door. Jack stopped outside each one and called softly.

"Princess Philomela! Are you there?"

But there was no reply at all until he reached the topmost room of all – and then an answer came, in a soft, eager voice.

"Yes, yes! I am here! Who is it?"

The door was locked and bolted – but the key was in the lock. Jack turned it, and then undid the bolts. He opened the door – and saw inside the room a beautiful little princess with long golden hair waving round her face, and the brightest blue eyes he had ever seen.

"Oh, oh, you've come to rescue me!"

cried Philomela, and she gave Jack and Mary a tight hug each. She saw the bunny and clapped her hands in delight.

"Why, you are dear little Whiskers, one of the bunnies that used to pull my carriage!" she said, and she lifted him up and kissed him. "I suppose you brought these children here to save me."

"We must go, Princess," said Jack. "The gnome knows we are here. He is looking for us downstairs. He may come up at any minute."

"Come along then," said Philomela. So they all began to creep down the stairs and at last came to the hall. No one was there. Not a sound was to be heard. Every door that led into the hall was shut.

"I say!" said Jack. "I don't remember which door led into the kitchen, do you?"

"We don't need to go that way," said Mary. "What about trying the front door?"

"No," said Jack. "It's too big and

heavy. It would make a noise. Let's go into one of the rooms; it doesn't much matter which one so long as the gnome isn't there, and then climb out of the window. That should be easy."

So they listened outside the nearest door, and, not hearing the tiniest sound from inside, they pushed open the door and slipped into the room. They ran to some curtains and pulled them aside to get at the windows – but alas – there were no windows at all!

Then they heard the sound of a key being turned in the lock – and looked round to see the Twisty Gnome looking at them with a very nasty grin.

"Ha!" he said. "So you thought you would rescue the Princess and all escape very nicely, did you? Well, you made a mistake, I'm afraid. I have four prisoners now, instead of one!"

He went to the middle of the floor, and pulled up a small wooden trap-door.

"Get down into my cellar," he said. "There is no escape from there. It is

dark and cold and full of spiders. You will enjoy a night or two there, I am sure!"

The Princess began to cry. Jack and Mary looked fierce, but could do nothing. The bunny slipped down into the cellar without a word.

When they were all in the dark, damp cellar, the gnome shut the trap-door with a bang and bolted it. They heard his footsteps going out of the room above.

"What are we going to do?" sobbed Philomela. "Oh, I am so frightened."

"So am I!" said Mary, wiping her eyes.

"There's no need to be," said the rabbit, in a soft voice. "I can rescue you all. I am a bunny, you know, and my paws are good for digging holes. This cellar is in the ground – there is earth all around. It will not take me long to dig my way out. Then I will fetch many more rabbits and we will all dig together."

"Splendid idea!" cried Jack. The

rabbit at once began to scrape in the earth. Soon he had made quite a tunnel, and the earth was piled in the cellar. In a few minutes he had disappeared – and before long he had fetched fifteen more rabbits, who all dug and scraped away valiantly.

"Now I think the tunnel is big enough," said the rabbit. And so it was. Jack, Mary and Philomela easily made their way up it, and came out at the side of the big castle!

"The rabbits have brought a carriage for you, Your Highness," said the little bunny – and there, sure enough, was a shining silver carriage! Four rabbits stood ready to pull it, and the Princess got in.

"You must come, too," she said to the children – but just as they were about to get in, a peculiar thing happened.

"Look at the moon!" cried the rabbit, and pointed to where the moon was slowly sinking down the sky.

Everyone looked. It was turning

bright yellow! Yes – there was no mistake about it. All its blue colour was fading – and even as they watched, it was all gone, and there was the moon, as bright yellow as a daffodil, filling the sky with light.

"The blue moon's gone," said the rabbit sadly. "It's gone – but we've rescued the Princess!"

A strange wind blew up at that moment and the children suddenly felt giddy. There came a loud humming noise. Jack and Mary sat down on the grass and shut their eyes, for they felt very strange.

After a while the humming noise died away – and they opened their eyes.

Will you believe it? They were back in their beds again! Yes, they were – both of them sitting up and gazing out of the window at the moon, which was yellow, and shining brightly!

"Mary!" cried Jack. "Did we dream it all?"

"No, we couldn't have," said Mary. "It

was all so real. The moon really *was* blue!"

"Well, tomorrow we will look for that trap-door again, where the bunny was," said Jack, lying down. "Then we will know for certain it was all true. How funny – Daddy will wonder where the stone bunny is gone, won't he?"

But do you know, when the morning came, the stone bunny was back again. Yes, he was – standing in the middle of the pond on the big flat stone just as before.

"But the trap-door is underneath him, Daddy," said Mary, earnestly, after she had told Daddy all about their very strange adventure. "It really is. Will you take him off the stone and see?"

"No," said Daddy. "He is cemented to the stone. I'm not going to move him. You dreamt it all!"

Well, isn't that a pity? If only Daddy would move the rabbit, and let the children find that trap-door again, they would know that it wasn't a dream. But Daddy won't.

Perhaps *you* will see a blue moon one day. If you do, wish a wish – for it is sure to come true, once in a blue moon!

The well-mannered scarecrow

Now once there was an old scarecrow who stood out in the fields by day and night, and flapped his jacket at all the rooks and jackdaws that came by.

He was a funny old creature. He had a turnip for a head, a scarf round his broomstick neck, an old ragged coat, and one leg. He had two arms made of sticks, and somebody had given him an old hat on his turnip head.

The scarecrow was very proud of this hat. There was a scarecrow in the next field, but he had no hat at all on *his* turnip head. And the one in the field on

the other side hadn't even a head – so the scarecrow felt quite proud to have not only a head, but a hat as well.

One night the brownies came into the field. They were really excited.

"The Queen is coming by this way tonight!" they said. "The Queen! Imagine that! She is so lovely. We will all come into this field, and cheer her and wave our hats."

"See that our brownie children are taught to curtsey, if they are girls, and to take off their hats if they are boys," said the head brownie.

"And even the rabbits must bow," said another brownie. "Good manners are very important. By the way, we must tell the toadstool brownie to be sure to wear his soldier's uniform and salute the Queen properly. He could put out his flag too. That would please her."

The scarecrow listened to all this, and felt quite excited himself.

"Will the Queen come anywhere near

me?" he called. "I'd so like to see her."

"Of course she will come near," said the head brownie. "And you must raise your hat politely to her. Don't forget."

"But I don't know how to raise my hat, and I shan't even know who the Queen is," said the scarecrow in a troubled voice. "My eyes are not awfully good, you know."

"Well, we will teach you how to raise your hat," said the brownies. "And you must do it when you hear us shout: 'Here comes Her Majesty the Queen!' Now, are you ready? You must bend your arm, take your hat off, and then put it back again. Now – one, two, three – here comes the Queen!"

The old scarecrow bent his stick of an arm, took hold of his hat, lifted it from his head – and dropped it on the ground!

"No, no," said the brownies. "That won't do. That really isn't polite, you know. Put your hat back on your *head*. Surely you know where your head is?"

"Well, I can't see it anywhere," said

the scarecrow, looking all round.

"Isn't he silly?" said the brownies to one another. "Of course he can't see his own head! Now, listen, Scarecrow – all you have to do is to put your hat back to where you lift it from. That's where your head is. Now then – one, two, three – here comes the Queen!"

The scarecrow tried again, and this time he managed not only to take off his hat but to put it back again – a little crooked, it is true, but still he managed it! The brownies praised him, and made him practise it again and again.

Well, when the Queen did come by that night, the scarecrow was as proud as could be because he was the only scarecrow who knew how to behave!

"The one over there hasn't a hat, so he can't raise it, and the other scarecrow hasn't even a head, so he doesn't know about the Queen," he thought happily. "This will be the proudest moment of my life."

Well, you should have seen the old

scarecrow when the Queen came by! He couldn't see well enough to make out who she was – but as soon as the brownies shouted, "Here comes the Queen!" his arm went up, he raised his hat very smartly, held it in the air for a moment, and then put it back again.

"What a clever and well-mannered scarecrow!" said the Queen's silvery voice as she passed. The scarecrow almost fell over with pride.

The brownies were pleased with him. "You did very well," they said. "We are proud of you."

Well, the old scarecrow is still standing out in the fields, his hat on his head, dreaming of the wonderful night when he raised that hat to the Queen. And now I am going to tell you a most peculiar thing.

If anyone goes into the field and shouts, "Here comes the Queen!" the scarecrow at once raises his hat most politely, and then puts it neatly back again on his head.

I can't tell you which scarecrow it is, because, as you know, scarecrows haven't names as we have. So if you think it *might* be the scarecrow in the fields near you, you'll know how to find out for certain. Shout out, "Here comes the Queen!" and see what happens.

I *do* hope he takes off his hat to you!

Nobody came to tea

There was once a lonely hare. He hadn't any friends, and he wanted some.

He talked to the scarecrow in the field, and the scarecrow gave him some advice.

"Ask people to tea. They like that. That is what children do. Give a party sometime, and ask all the creatures to come."

It was summer-time when the scarecrow told the hare this. The hare felt excited. "It will take me a long time to get things for the party," he said. "I will ask everyone for the last week in October. Then I shall have plenty of time to collect food for my guests."

He asked the little dormouse, who was delighted. He asked the prickly hedgehog, and he was very pleased. He asked both the frog and the toad, and as they were cousins they said they would come together.

"That's four," said the hare. "Now, who's next to be asked? Oh yes – I'll ask the lizard and the snake, and I'll ask the little black bat too. He will enjoy a party. I must try to get some beetles for him."

So he asked them all, and they said yes, they would all come to tea with him and be friends.

"Seven guests," the hare told the scarecrow. "It's a *real* party, isn't it?"

Well, the day of the party came. The hare had collected food for every one of his guests, and he set it all out in his field.

Then he waited for his visitors to come. But nobody came to tea. Nobody at all. The dormouse didn't turn up, and neither did the hedgehog. The frog and

toad were not to be seen. The lizard didn't come frisking along, and no gliding, silent snake came to tea. Even the little black bat was missing too.

The hare was sad. "Nobody likes me," he said. "Nobody has come to tea. They said they would – but they were making fun of me. They didn't mean to come."

"What's the matter?" said the rabbit, who was passing by. The hare told him. The rabbit laughed loudly.

"Silly hare! The dormouse is down at the bottom of the ivy-roots, asleep. The hedgehog is snoring in a hole in the bank over there. The frog is at the bottom of the pond, and the toad asleep under a stone. The lizard is in a hollow stump, and the snake sleeps with his brothers in an old tree. The little black bat is asleep too, hanging upside down in the barn."

"Asleep! Why are they all asleep?" said the hare.

"Well, they always sleep the winter away – didn't you know that?" said the rabbit scornfully. "It's no good having a party at this time of year. But cheer up – I and my family will come if you like. We shan't eat the tea you've got ready – but we'll all play games."

So they did, and the hare enjoyed himself after all. But none of his real guests came to the party – they wouldn't wake up till the spring-time.

Slowcoach Sammy

Slowcoach Sammy belonged to a family of brownies, and you can guess why he had such a funny name. He *was* such a slowcoach! He was last in everything, and his mother, Mrs Trot-About, got quite cross with him.

"You're always last, Sammy," she said. "I call the others, and they come running at once. But you stay behind and make me feel so cross."

Poor old Slowcoach Sammy! He missed the bus when he went shopping. He missed the train when Mrs Trot-About took the family to see Aunt Twinkle. He even missed the elephant when he went to the zoo, so he couldn't have his ride.

One day his mother called to all her family, "Come with me. I want you to do some gardening. I have lettuce, mustard and cress seeds, and we will plant them all in our garden so that we shall have plenty to eat in the summer."

Tickle came running. Humps rushed up. Jinky came round the corner at top speed. Ricky arrived panting. But Slowcoach Sammy wasn't to be seen, as usual.

"He's watching a spider making its web at the front gate," said Tickle.

"Sammy, Sammy, Sammy! Hurry up or you won't have time to do any gardening!" cried Mrs Trot-About. "I've only twenty minutes to spare to help you all plant your seeds."

But Slowcoach Sammy didn't hurry. He watched the spider till she had finished her web. Then he watched a worm wriggling out of a hole. Then he watched a bird flying right up into the sky. And at last he got to his mother and his brothers and sisters.

But they had finished their gardening and were picking up their spades to put them back into the shed.

"What a slowcoach you are, Sammy!" said Mrs Trot-About. "I called you ages ago! Now we have finished, and all the seeds are planted."

"I want to plant some seeds too," said Sammy.

"Well, you can't. The others have planted them all – there they are, neatly labelled in rows," said his mother, waving her spade to the garden-beds.

"I *do* want to plant some seeds!" wept Sammy. "I want some plants of my own too. I *do* want to plant some seeds!"

"It's no use making that noise," said his mother. "You should have come when you were called. There are no more seeds at all."

Sammy went off to cry in the playroom. He hunted in the cupboard to see if there *were* any packets of seeds left. And at last he came to a little packet that rattled when he shook it.

He opened it. Inside lay a great many tiny coloured round things.

"Seeds!" said Slowcoach Sammy, delighted. "Seeds that everybody else has forgotten. I'll go and plant them straightaway, and won't the others look blue when they see I *have* got seeds coming up after all!"

Well, if Sammy had looked closely at that packet, he would have seen that they were tiny beads belonging to his sister Jinky! But he didn't. He just hurried out to plant them.

He made little holes along his garden-bed and shook the beads inside. He covered them up well. He watered them, and patted down the ground nicely. He was very pleased with himself.

"They can call me Slowcoach all they like, but they'll be surprised when they see how much nicer my seeds are than theirs!" said Sammy to himself. "My word, with seeds coloured as brightly as that I ought to have flowers all colours of the rainbow!"

Well, the other seeds began to come up, showing a green mist in the beds – but Slowcoach Sammy's didn't peep through at all! He went out to look twenty times a day, but it wasn't any use – he didn't see a single green head coming through the soft brown earth.

He was *so* disappointed. The seeds of the others grew and grew – but Sammy's didn't come up at all. (And *I'm* not really surprised, are you?)

Mrs Trot-About was sorry to see Sammy so unhappy about his seeds. He had told her that he had found a forgotten packet in the cupboard, and she thought they were mustard and cress or lettuce. She couldn't *think* why they didn't come up.

"I shall dig them up and see what's the matter with them," said Slowcoach Sammy to the others.

"Maybe they are slowcoaches like you!" said Jinky. They all came with him and watched him dig up his bed.

He turned up heaps of the little round coloured things and picked them out of the earth.

"Just look!" he said. "They haven't put out any root or shoot or bud or leaf! What bad seeds they are!"

Then the others began to laugh. How they laughed! "What's the matter?" asked Sammy, in surprise. "Do you think my seeds are so funny?"

"Yes, we do!" laughed Ricky. "What did you expect to grow from those seeds, Sammy? Necklace flowers and bracelet buds? They are tiny little *beads*!"

Poor Sammy Slowcoach! He stood and stared at his bead-seeds and tears trickled down his red cheeks. No wonder they wouldn't grow! He had planted beads!

"Never mind, Sammy, you can share my lettuces," said kind Jinky.

"It's not the same to share," said Sammy. "I want seeds of my own."

"Then you mustn't be such a little

slowcoach next time," said his mother. "We'll try and help you not to be."

And what do you think his family say to him when they see Sammy being slow? They say, "Hi, Sammy! Your beads will never grow unless you hurry up!"

Then, my goodness, how he hurries and scurries!

The tail of Bup the bunny

There was once a bunny called Bup. He was very vain and longed for everyone to look at him and admire him. His whiskers were long, his ears were big, and his fur was thick. The only thing he didn't like was his tail.

It was just a furry blob, like all rabbits' tails. Bup wanted a big tail, one like Bushy the squirrel's, or a long one like Puss Cat. It was horrid to have a little bobtail that nobody took any notice of at all.

Then, one day, when he was out in the woods, he found a lovely long white tail. It had belonged to a toy cat that a little boy had taken for a walk. The tail had caught in a bramble and fallen off, so

the little boy had left it there.

Bup picked it up and looked at it. Here was exactly the kind of tail he had so often wanted. He would take it home, try it on, and see how it looked!

So off he went clippitty-clippitty through the wood, and ran down his hole. When he was safely down there, he tied the long white tail on to him, and then looked over his shoulder to see what it was like.

"My!" he said. "I look grand! Yes, I do! I shall have this tail for my own, and pretend to everyone that it is real. No one will know, and they will all admire me, and be jealous! I shall be the only rabbit with a long tail!"

He stayed in his hole for a few days, and when his friends came to see what was the matter, he put his head out and answered them very proudly.

"I am growing a long tail," he said. "I hear it's quite the fashion now. It's only half-grown yet, but as soon as it is full-grown, I'll show it to you."

Well, all the rabbits were most astonished. They asked each other whether anyone had heard of a long-tailed bunny before, but no one ever had. They began to think that Bup was making fun of them, so they waited anxiously for the day to come when he would come and play with them again.

On the seventh day Bup the bunny came out of his hole. He had tied the toy cat's tail very firmly on to him, so that it quite hid his own bobtail. As he lolloped out of his hole, all the rabbits cried out in surprise.

"Yes, he's grown a long tail! Yes, he has! Come and look, everybody! Bup has a long tail!"

Not only the rabbits came to see, but the foxes and weasels, sparrows and thrushes, hedgehogs and moles. The foxes and weasels were not allowed to come too near, for the rabbits hated them, but they came quite near enough to see the wonderful long tail.

How proud Bup was! He hopped

about here and there, showing off his long tail, enjoying all the cries of surprise and envy.

"How did you do it, Bup?" asked the other rabbits. "Tell us, and we will do the same."

Bup knew quite well that they *couldn't* do the same because his was only a pretend tail. But he couldn't tell them that, of course, so he sat down and looked very wise.

"All you've got to do," he said, "is to sit at home in your burrow, think about tails for seven days, and then at the end of that time you will have one as good as mine."

Well, the silly rabbits believed him! Off they all went to their burrows, and sat at home for seven days thinking of nothing but tails. But alas for them! When they came out again their tails were as short as ever! They were dreadfully disappointed.

"You are stupid creatures," said Bup, curling his whiskers. "I am the cleverest of all of you. Why don't you make me your king? It would be nice for you to have a long-tailed rabbit for king, wouldn't it?"

Now, not many rabbits liked Bup, for he was so vain. But he was so determined to be king that at last they thought they had better make him their chief.

So they all set out to go to Breezy Hill where they held their important meetings. They sat round in a ring, with Bup in the middle, and the oldest rabbit by him.

"Friends," said the oldest rabbit. "You are met together today to decide whether Bup the bunny shall be your king or not. He is the only long-tailed rabbit in our town. We have all tried to grow tails like his and we cannot. Therefore it seems as if he must be the cleverest among us. Shall we make him king?"

But before the listening rabbits could answer, a red fox came slinking up. He had smelt the rabbits from far off, and had come to see if he could pick one of them up for his dinner. They saw him coming over the hilltop, and with one frightened look they took to their heels and fled.

Bup fled too. His long tail dragged on the ground behind him, but he had forgotten all about it. All he thought of was his hole, his lovely, safe, cosy hole! If only he could get there before the red fox caught him!

The fox chose to chase Bup, for he was fat and could not run quite so fast as the others. So off he went after poor Bup.

All the other rabbits reached their holes safely, and popped their heads out to watch the race. Nearer and nearer the fox came till he was almost on top of Bup. Then he suddenly made a snatch at the bunny's long tail – and got it in his mouth!

"Oh! Oh! Now Bup is caught!" cried all the watching rabbits.

But the string that tied the long tail

on to Bup suddenly broke, and Bup raced on free, whilst the astonished fox stopped still with the tail in his mouth.

"My! Oh my!" sang out the rabbits. "Why, Bup's got a short tail as well as a long tail! Just look! There's his little bobtail just like ours!"

So there was, quite plain to see, as Bup ran helter-skelter for his hole. Down he popped in safety, and lay there panting. How glad he was that his long tail had only been a pretend one!

The fox gave one chew at the pretend tail and then blew it out of his mouth. Off he went in disgust. When he was safely out of sight, the rabbits all came crowding out to see the tail. They soon found out that it was nothing but a toy cat's tail, and how cross they were!

"To think that we all sat in our burrows for seven days, thinking of nothing but tails!" cried the oldest rabbit. "And we nearly made that wicked rabbit our king!"

"And how foolish we should have been, if we *had* grown long tails!" said another. "Why, the fox would catch us easily, if our tails were any longer!"

"Where's that stupid Bup Bunny?" cried all the rabbits. "Let us go and find him!"

So off they went to Bup's burrow, and dragged him out. They gave him a good scolding so that both his ears drooped, and his eyes filled with tears.

And that was the end of Bup being so vain. If ever he showed any signs of being proud again, someone would say to him, "Well, Bup? Have you grown another long tail yet?"

And then Bup would go very red, and run away!

The tale of Tinker the pup

I am a puppy dog, and my name is Tinker. I am in disgrace, and I have been put in the corner; it is a great shame.

"Tinker," my mistress said, "you have been a very naughty little dog all day long! I am ashamed of you!"

Well *I* don't think I have been at all naughty, and I am just going to tell you all I have done today, then you will know that my mistress is quite mistaken. I am a very good dog.

I woke up at six o'clock, and got out of my basket. I sleep with my master and mistress, and my basket is put in the corner of their bedroom. I felt a bit lonely, so I jumped up on the bed.

The eiderdown tickled my nose, so I bit a big hole in it, the nasty thing – and oh, do you know, it was full of the most exciting little feathers! They all came blowing out when I breathed on them. So I spent a lovely time chasing them, and biting them. I thought my mistress would be pleased when she woke up and saw how many I had caught.

But she wasn't! No, not a bit! She was *ever* so cross! She said I had spoilt her eiderdown.

So I went downstairs to the cook. She was pleased to see me, and gave me a pat and a biscuit. I licked her hand, and then tried to fight her feet, but she wouldn't let me.

Soon I found a scrubbing-brush on the floor, and didn't I have a game with it! I had torn all the bristles out before Cook found me.

"That was a fine brush you put down for me to play with," I said to her. But would you believe it, she was very angry.

"You wicked little dog!" she said. "Fancy ruining a lovely new brush like that!"

After breakfast I went upstairs to sniff round the bedrooms. I found a nice soft slipper under my master's bed. So I pulled it out, and looked at it.

"Play with me!" I said. But it wouldn't. No matter how much I asked it to, it wouldn't play at all. I thought it was very horrid of it, and I gave it a bite just to show it what I thought. But still it wouldn't play.

Then I got really fierce and shook it hard between my teeth. "I'll teach you not to play with me, you horrid, impolite thing!" I said.

I did teach it. It was all in bits before I had finished, and I'm sure it was very sorry it had been so horrid to me. Then – oh, dear! – my mistress came along.

"My lovely bedroom slipper!" she cried. "Oh, you bad little puppy! You've nibbled it all to bits!"

I tried to tell my mistress that that

was a good punishment for impolite slippers, but she wouldn't listen. She took me by the scruff of my neck and dragged me downstairs.

"I'll smack you the very next time you are naughty today!" she said, and she shut me into the kitchen.

Well, no sooner had I got there, than I smelt the *loveliest* smell I have ever smelt. It was SAUSAGES.

There was a long string of them on the table.

"I expect Cook has brought one for me," I said to myself. "Well, I'm hungry, so I'll have it now."

I took the end one into my mouth – but they were all joined together, so the whole string fell down on to the floor.

"I'd better take my sausage into the yard in case Cook remembers about the scrubbing brush," I thought. So I tried to drag my one sausage into the backyard – but all the other sausages came too. I couldn't make them stop coming.

"Well, if you *really* must come," I said. "I warn you, you may be eaten."

I thought that would make them scurry away – but it didn't. So I ate them all, every one. Weren't they lovely!

But oh, Cook was crosser than ever I've seen her before. She took up a broom and chased me with it. I scuttled out into the garden as fast as I could go.

"What horrid people live in my house!" I thought to myself. "I've a good mind not to live here any more."

Just then I heard a funny sort of noise, and in the next garden I saw a lot of fluffy yellow chicks. They were cheeping loudly, and making such a noise.

"Be quiet," I growled. "I have a headache, and I want to go to sleep."

Well, those disobedient little chicks wouldn't take a bit of notice of me, so I squeezed my way through the hedge and went to tell them what I thought of them.

I ran at them, and they all scurried away, cheeping loudly. I thought this was rather a nice game, so I chased them all over the place. And then – my goodness – the fiercest old hen came up and was *ever* so rude to me.

She flew at me, and pecked me on the nose three times. I couldn't seem to get away from her. But at last I did, and I squeezed through the hedge as quick as anything, with that horrid old hen pecking me all the time.

"It's no wonder your chicks are bad-mannered if they've got a mother like you!" I said. Then I ran up the garden as fast as I could.

I hadn't gone very far when I remembered that I had buried a bone somewhere yesterday. So I began to look for it. There were a lot of those red, blue, and yellow things about – flowers, my mistress calls them – and they were in my way. So I scraped a whole lot up, but still I couldn't find my bone.

Then I suddenly remembered where I

had buried it, and I ran to the bed. The gardener had put dozens of little green plants in it – just like him to use my bone-bed for that – so I had to dig them all up.

It was just whilst I was doing that – and making a very good job of it too – that my master came out and saw me.

"You young rascal!" he said. Then he carried me indoors to my mistress.

"He's dug up half the garden," said Master. "Put him in the corner, and tie him up for the rest of the day, my dear. He'll dig up the house next."

So here I am in the corner, and nobody will speak to me because I am in disgrace. But *I* don't think I have been so very bad, do you?

Sneezing powder

Once upon a time there lived a brownie called Smarty. He kept a little shop in Hallo Town, in which he sold jars of honey, fine yellow lemons, and big yellow pills that helped to cure colds.

In the winter-time Smarty did a fine trade, for anyone who had a cold came to buy his honey, his juicy lemons, and his cold-pills. Then they would go home, squeeze the lemons into a glass, put in hot water and sugar and a spoonful or two of Smarty's golden honey, take a cold-pill, and go to bed – and lo and behold, next morning they were cured!

But in the summer-time nobody seemed to have a cold at all. It was most annoying for Smarty. Instead of thinking of selling something else, such as ice-creams or cool lemon drinks, Smarty still went on hoping that people would have colds and buy his cold-cure. So he wasn't quite as smart as his name, was he?

He was quite smart enough to think out a naughty trick, though!

"If only I could *make* people think they had a cold, they would come and buy my honey and lemons and pills," thought Smarty. "If only they would sneeze or cough just as they passed my shop, it would be so easy for me to say, 'Dear me! You are getting a cold! Buy my cold-cure before you are very bad!' But nobody ever sneezes outside my shop."

Smarty sat and thought for a bit, and then he grinned all over his sly little face. He slapped his knee in delight. He had thought of a wonderful idea!

"I'll go and buy some sneezing powder from old Dame Flap!" he said to himself.

"And I'll put some into my pepper-pot and shake it out of my bedroom window whenever anyone passes! Then they will sneeze hard, and perhaps come and buy my goods."

So off he went to buy the sneezing powder. He paid Dame Flap a silver coin for a boxful and she wrapped it up for him. It was a strange powder, rather like fine green flour, and it had a strange smell.

Smarty ran home with it. He emptied some into his pepper-pot and slipped upstairs to his bedroom window, which was just over his shop. He leaned out in excitement. Was anybody coming?

Yes – here was Old Man Shuffle! Smarty waited till he was underneath the window and then he shook out some of the powder. It went on Old Man Shuffle's nose, and he stopped. He took out his big blue handkerchief and held it to his nose.

"Whooosh!" he sneezed. "A-whoosh!"

"Hi, Old Man Shuffle, you've got a

dreadful cold!" called Smarty. "Come into my shop and get some honey and lemons and pills!"

So in shuffled the old fellow, thinking it was very lucky that he should be outside Smarty's shop just when his cold had begun. He bought a jar of honey, two lemons, and a box of yellow pills. Smarty grinned. He ran up to his bedroom again.

"Ah! Here are Mr Twiddle and his wife!" chuckled Smarty. He shook his pepper-pot over them. They stopped and fumbled for their hankies.

"Er-tish-oo!" said Mr Twiddle loudly.

"Ish-ish-ish!" sneezed Mrs Twiddle politely into her handkerchief.

"ER-TISH-OOO!" went Mr Twiddle.

"Not so much noise, Twiddle," said Mrs Twiddle. "Ish-ish-ish-ish! Dear me! We are beginning colds, I think. Look, let's buy some honey and lemons, and maybe we'll stop our colds from getting worse."

So into Smarty's shop they went and

bought what they wanted, much to Smarty's delight. As soon as they had gone, he popped upstairs again with his pepper-pot full of sneezing powder.

He made Twinkle the pixie sneeze and buy honey and pills. He made Mr Meddle sneeze so strongly that his hat flew on to the roof and he had to get a ladder to fetch it. He made Dame Winks sneeze twelve times, and at the end her bonnet was right over her nose and she couldn't see where she was going at all.

Oh, Smarty had plenty of fun that day, and he made plenty of money, too! But when everyone found that they had no cold at all when they got home, and didn't need the honey and lemons, they were rather puzzled. They talked about it to one another, and they found that all of them had begun their sneezing fits outside Smarty's shop.

"Very nice for Smarty!" said Mr Meddle. "Let us go along and see what we can see."

So they all went back towards Smarty's shop, and peeped round the corner. And they saw Smarty leaning out of his bedroom window, pepper-pot in hand!

"Aha!" said Old Man Shuffle angrily. "So that's his trick, is it! Come along, everybody!"

They all went into Smarty's shop. Smarty hurried down to serve them. Mrs Twiddle was waiting for him. She snatched the pepper-pot out of his pocket and shook it all over Smarty.

"Colds are catching today!" she said. "Sneeze, Smarty, sneeze! Dear, dear! You must have caught our colds."

"Whoosh!" said Smarty. "Atish-oo! Ish-ish-ish! Osha-whoosh! Tish-oo!"

Mrs Twiddle emptied all the sneezing powder over him. My goodness, Smarty simply could *not* stop sneezing! It was dreadful!

"By the time you've finished I guess you'll want to buy a pot of your own honey, a dozen lemons, and a box of pills!" said Mr Twiddle, laughing. "Goodbye, Smarty. It serves you right!"

They all went out, giggling and chuckling, and they could hear Smarty's sneezes all the way down the road.

Poor Smarty! He sneezed all that day and all that night, and by that time his nose and throat and eyes were so sore that he had to take two jars of honey, six lemons, and two of his own pills to cure himself!

Now he has shut up his shop and gone out selling ice-creams. And a very much better idea, too, in the summer – don't you think so?

Trundle goes out to tea

If ever you go to the little brownie village of Tucked-Away you will notice a curious thing. You will see that every brownie wears a green leaf sewn into his tight little breeches, just over his right knee-cap. And you are sure to wonder why.

Well, I will tell you the reason, because I'm sure you won't like to ask the brownies. We shall have to go right back to the day when Trundle the brownie went out to tea.

Now Trundle didn't live in the village of Tucked-Away. Oh dear me no, *he* lived in the town of Very-Big, where everything was up-to-date, and all the brownies wore the very latest thing in

111

pointed caps, and knew exactly how many buttons should go on a coat, and important things like that.

The brownies of Tucked-Away were very old-fashioned, although they tried hard not to be. As Trundle said, they simply did not *know* how to dress. They wore fifteen buttons down their coats when everyone in Very-Big was only wearing fourteen, and had five pockets instead of two.

The village of Tucked-Away thought a lot of Very-Big, and whenever a visitor from the town paid them a visit they were very much excited. They made everything as nice as ever they could and tried their hardest to show the visitor that they could do things quite as well as Very-Big.

So you can imagine that when Trundle said he would go and have tea with his cousin in Tucked-Away there was great excitement. Trundle was a very up-to-date brownie, and always dressed just so. Jinks, his cousin, couldn't keep the news to himself when he got Trundle's letter, and he rushed round to all his friends to tell them that a brownie from Very-Big was coming to tea the very next Friday.

"I'll have a tea-party," he said, "and you must all come, dressed in your very best things, and we'll show Trundle that the village of Tucked-Away can be just as well dressed as the town of Very-Big!"

So everyone began to take out best suits and sponge them and iron them. They polished up the buttons, and put clean handkerchiefs in the breast pockets all ready for the tea-party.

Jinks made all sorts of scones and cakes and bought three different sorts of jam from the jam-woman. He made a yellow jelly and a red one, and when the day came you should have seen his tea-table. It was enough to make your mouth water! The brownies going by his cottage in the morning peeped in through the window, and what they saw made them long for the afternoon to come.

Jinks had asked everybody to come at four o'clock. Trundle was coming at half-past three, and Jinks thought that his visitor would just have time to wash and polish up his shoes before all the guests came.

At half-past two Trundle started out from the town of Very-Big to walk to Tucked-Away, which was four miles away. He had on his newest suit, and a fine new hat with a red feather in it. He liked his cousin Jinks and he was looking forward to the tea-party, for he hadn't had much dinner.

He went merrily along, whistling a tune, walking in the shade, for the sun was hot. He was very nearly at Tucked-Away when a dreadful thing happened. Trundle caught his foot on a root and tumbled right over! And when he got up again, he found that he had torn a big hole in his nice red breeches, just over his right knee-cap!

"Oh, my!" said Trundle, in dismay. "Now isn't that unfortunate? Never mind, Jinks is sure to offer me a needle and thread when I get to his house, and I'll just have to mend it up as best I can."

He took a green leaf, and tucked it into the hole, for his knee was grazed and bleeding a little, and he didn't want his socks to be stained. Then he went on his way again, and soon arrived at Jinks' little cottage.

Jinks was at the door to greet him, and took him indoors to wash after his dusty walk. Jinks looked at his cousin's suit carefully, and decided that his own was just as fashionable – and then he caught sight of the green leaf stuck over Trundle's knee-cap.

"Dear me!" he thought. "*That's* a new idea, surely! I suppose it's a sort of trimming. Dear, dear, dear, and not one of my guests will be in the fashion now, for none of us has got green-leaf trimming on his right knee! What can I do? There's half an hour before the

115

tea-party begins, so perhaps there's just time to send little notes round and tell everyone to wear a green leaf sewn on to their right knee."

"The guests won't be here for a little while, Trundle," said Jinks to his visitor. "Would you like to go and sit out in the garden, and rest after your long walk?"

So whilst Trundle was resting in the garden, Jinks hurriedly wrote lots of little notes, and gave them to his servant to deliver.

"Please be sure to wear a green leaf as trimming, sewn over your right knee-cap," said each note. "It is the latest fashion in Very-Big. Trundle is wearing one this afternoon."

You can guess that when the guests received these notes they all rushed out in a great hurry, and got green leaves to sew on to their right knee-caps. That took time, so they were all a bit late when they arrived.

Trundle fell fast asleep in the garden,

and when he awoke he saw the first of the guests coming in at the gate.

"My goodness!" he cried. "I haven't mended this hole in the knee of my breeches! Whatever will the guests think of me?"

He got up to go and shake hands with the little brownie coming into the garden. When he saw the first one, he was very much astonished.

"What an extraordinary thing!" he thought. "Here's another brownie who must have tumbled down and torn his suit too, because he's got a green leaf over his knee-cap like me!"

His astonishment was even greater when he saw that the second brownie had a green leaf over his knee as well. And the third one, and the fourth! *And* his cousin, who certainly hadn't when he had met him at the door!

"Bless us, they've *all* got green leaves on their knees!" thought Trundle in the greatest amazement. "Am I in a dream, or what?"

He thought he really couldn't be, for the cakes tasted just like real ones, and as for the jelly, it was simply lovely. All the brownies seemed so very pleased with themselves, and looked proudly, first at Trundle's leaf-trimmed knee and then at their own.

Trundle was more and more puzzled, until a little brownie suddenly helped him to solve the mystery.

"Such a pretty new fashion, the leaf-trimming on the knee, isn't it?" said the brownie to Trundle. "As you see, Tucked-Away is not behind Very-Big in fashion!"

"*Well!*" thought Trundle. "Why in the world do they think that there's a fashion of that sort in Very-Big? There certainly isn't and never will be! I wonder – I wonder – is it possible that Jinks thought I was wearing this leaf as a sort of trimming and didn't guess I'd tumbled down and torn my breeches? He certainly didn't offer me a needle and thread to mend it with as I thought he would. I suppose he sent round notes to all the guests to tell them to wear leaves too, so as to be in the fashion! Oh, dear me, what a joke!"

Trundle had guessed quite rightly, and it made him smile to look round the tea-party and see everyone proudly wearing leaves over their right knees, thinking that they were very fashionable indeed.

"I mustn't let them know that there's no such fashion," he thought. "They would be so terribly upset – but, oh dear, if this isn't the very funniest thing that ever I saw!"

Trundle tried his hardest not to laugh, for he was a kind-hearted little brownie, but for once in a way he was quite glad when the party came to an end. He wanted to laugh and laugh!

And all the way home he *did* laugh! You should just have heard him! Even the bunnies peeped out of their holes and laughed too, although they didn't know why!

From that day to this the village of Tucked-Away has kept to the fashion — so if ever you meet a brownie wearing a green leaf on his right knee, you will know where he comes from!

It grew and it grew

Once little Fibs, the pixie, told his mother a story. He often didn't tell the truth, and it made her sad.

Fibs had been playing with his ball in the garden and it had gone on to the rose-bed. He had gone to get it and had trodden all over the bed and broken some roses off.

"Oh, Fibs – did *you* do that?" cried his mother.

"No. It was Frisky, the dog," said Fibs.

"Then he's very naughty," said his mother. "Go and find him and tie him up."

Fibs didn't want to do that. He liked Frisky. But he ran out and pretended to look for him. "Mother, he's frightened and he's gone into the next door garden," he said, when he came back. That was another fib, of course. That first fib was certainly growing!

"Oh dear!" said his mother in dismay. "Dame Pitpat has hens, and if Frisky chases them she will be so cross. Go and ask her if she will let you go into her garden and catch him."

Fibs ran off. He went next door and pretended to ring the bell. Nobody came, of course, because he *hadn't* rung the bell. He ran back to his mother.

"Dame Pitpat is out," he said. "I rang and I rang, and nobody came. But never mind – Frisky ran out of her garden and he's gone down the road."

"Well, that's good," said his mother. "But I shall certainly tie him up when he comes in."

She went into the garden to hang up some clothes. Fibs heaved a sigh of relief. Perhaps now he needn't tell another fib.

Soon his mother came hurrying in. "Fibs, Fibs, where are you? There's a burglar in Dame Pitpat's house. There must be, because you said she was out. I distinctly saw someone at the upstairs window. You go and ask old Rappy to come along and find out!"

Fibs sighed. Oh dear, oh dear! It was all beginning again! He ran out to Mr Rappy's house, but he didn't knock at the door. He just stood there – then he went back again to his mother.

"Mr Rappy says he's got a very bad leg and he can't come. He says you must have been mistaken. There can't be a burglar in Dame Pitpat's house."

"How does *he* know?" cried his mother. "Well, I shall send you to Mr Plod, the policeman, then. *Somebody* must come and get the burglar next door! Run, Fibs, run and get Mr Plod at once."

Fibs couldn't think *what* to do! He was standing there, wondering what to say, when his mother gave a loud cry. "Oh! There *is* Mr Plod! Look, by the front gate. Go and get him at once!"

Fibs went out slowly, hoping that Mr Plod would have gone by the time he reached the gate. His mother ran out crossly. "Why don't you hurry, Fibs? Mr Plod, Mr Plod! There's a robber in Dame Pitpat's house!"

Mr Plod turned in surprise. "Is there really, Ma'am? Then I'll climb in at a window and catch him right away!"

And in no time at all there was Mr Plod climbing in at a window of Dame Pitpat's house! There was nobody downstairs so he went upstairs very quietly and walked into the bedroom.

Somebody screamed and sat up in bed! It was Dame Pitpat herself, having a little rest. "Oh, what is it? Who is it? Why, it's Mr Plod! What do you want, Mr Plod?"

"Well, I was told there was a burglar in the house," said Mr Plod. "Little Fibs next door was sent to you with a message and he came back and said

you were out, and then his mother saw somebody moving in the upstairs room, and . . ."

"Bless us all! I wasn't out!" said Dame Pitpat. "He couldn't have rung the bell or I'd have heard it. It was me that Fibs' mother saw upstairs. Please go away, Mr Plod, and leave me in peace."

Mr Plod went down and told Fibs' mother and she was really very puzzled. She was even more puzzled when she saw Mr Rappy coming out of his house with his stick under his arm, walking quickly to catch the bus.

"Why, Mr Rappy! When Fibs asked you for help just now, you told him you couldn't come because you had a very bad leg!" cried Fibs' mother, looking very amazed.

"Nonsense!" said Mr Rappy. "He never came to ask me anything at all. Just one of his tales!" He rapped with his stick on the fence. "He wants a taste of this – then he wouldn't tell so many stories!"

"Fibs! You didn't go to Mr Rappy – and I don't believe you went to Dame Pitpat's either!" said his mother, shocked. "And I don't suppose Frisky was in her garden. Where *is* he then? Frisky, Frisky!"

A loud barking came from upstairs. Fibs' mother ran up and opened a door. Inside the room was Frisky, wagging his tail.

"Why, he's been here all the time," said Fibs' mother. "He's been asleep on his rug. He *couldn't* have run over the bed and broken the roses. Then who did, Fibs? Answer me that!"

She went out to the bed – and there she saw the footprints quite clearly. They were Fibs', of course.

"You horrid mean little pixie!" she cried. "Blaming poor Frisky – telling me he had run away next door – and saying that Dame Pitpat was out and Mr Rappy had a bad leg. Don't you know that one fib leads to another and always brings trouble in the end? Well, trouble is coming to *you*, Fibs!"

Poor Fibs! His mother told the truth – it was ages before he was allowed out to play again. It's strange how one fib leads to another, isn't it? Fibs knows that now and he'll never forget it!

Tale of a teddy and a mouse

The new teddy bear was very small indeed. The toys stared at him when he first came into the playroom, wondering what he was.

"Good gracious, I believe you're a teddy bear!" said Amelia Jane, the naughty doll. "I thought you were a peculiar-shaped mouse."

"Well, I'm not," said the small bear sharply, and he pressed himself in the middle. "*Grrrrrr*! Hear my growl? Well, no mouse can growl, it can only squeak."

"Yes. You're a bear all right," said the pink rabbit. "I hear you've come to live with us. Well, I'll show you your place in the toy cupboard, right at the back."

"I don't like being at the back, it's too dark," said the little bear. "I'll be at the front here, by this big brick-box."

"Oh, no, you won't. That's *my* place when I want to sit in the toy cupboard," said Amelia Jane. "And let me tell you this, small bear, if you live with us, you'll have to take on lots of little bits of work. We all do. You'll have

to wind up the clockwork clown when he runs down, you'll have to clean the dolls' house windows, and you'll have to help the engine-driver polish his big red train."

"Dear me, I don't think I want to do any of those things," said the bear. "I'm lazy. I don't like working."

"Well, you'll just have to," said Amelia Jane. "Otherwise you won't get any of the biscuit crumbs that the children drop on the floor, you won't get any of the sweets in the toy sweet shop – and we're allowed some every week – and you won't come to any parties."

"Pooh!" said the bear and stalked off to pick up some beads out of the bead-box and thread himself a necklace.

"He's vain as well as lazy," said the rabbit in disgust. "Hey, Bear, what's your name? Or are you too lazy to have one?"

"My name is Sidney Gordon Eustace," said the bear, haughtily. "And I don't like being called Sid."

"Sid!" yelled all the toys at once, and the bear looked furious. He turned his head away, and went on threading the beads.

"Sidney Gordon Eustace!" said the clown, with a laugh. "I guess he gave himself those names. No sensible child would ever call a teddy bear that. Huh!"

The bear was not much use in the playroom. He just would *not* do any of the jobs there at all. He went surprisingly deaf when anyone called to him to come and clean or polish or sweep. He would pretend to be asleep, or just walk about humming a little tune as if nobody was calling his name at all. It was most annoying.

"Sidney! Come and shake the mats for the dolls' house dolls!" the pink rabbit called. No answer from Sidney at all.

"SIDNEY, come here! You're not as deaf as all that."

The bear never even turned his head. "Hey, Sidney Gordon Eustace, come and do your jobs," yelled the rabbit.

No answer.

"All right!" shouted the rabbit, angrily, "you shan't have that nice big crumb of chocolate biscuit we found under the table this morning."

It was always the same whenever there was a job to be done. "Sidney, come here!"

But Sidney never came. He never did one single thing for any of the toys.

"What are we going to do about him?" said the big teddy bear. "I'd like to spank him – but he's too quick for me. Amelia Jane, can't you think of a good idea?"

"Oh, yes," said Amelia at once. "I know what we'll do. We'll get Sidney the mouse to come and do the things that Sidney the bear should do – and he shall have all the crumbs and titbits that the bear should have. He won't like that – a common little house-mouse getting all his treats!"

"Dear me, is the house-mouse's name

Sidney, too?" asked the rabbit in surprise. "I never knew that before. When we want him we usually go to his hole and shout 'Mouse', and he comes."

"Well, I'll go and shout 'Sidney'," said Amelia Jane, "and you'll see – he'll come!" So she went to the little hole at the bottom of the wall near the bookcase and shouted down it.

"Sidney! Sid-Sid-Sidney! We want you."

The little bear, of course, didn't turn round – *he* wasn't going to come when his name was called. But someone very small came scampering up the passage to the entrance of the hole.

It was the tiny brown house-mouse, with bright black eyes and twitching whiskers.

"Ah, Sidney," said Amelia Jane. "Will you just come and shake the mats in the dolls' house, please? They are very dusty. We'll give you a big chocolate biscuit crumb and a drink of lemonade out of the little teapot if you will."

"Can I drink out of the spout?" said the tiny mouse, pleased. "I like drinking out of the spout."

"Yes, of course," said Amelia Jane.

The little mouse set about shaking the mats vigorously, and the job was soon done.

"Isn't Sidney wonderful?" said Amelia in a loud voice to the others. "Sidney the mouse, I mean, of course, not silly Sidney the bear. He wouldn't have the strength to shake mats like that, poor thing. Sidney, here's your chocolate biscuit crumb and there's the teapot full of lemonade."

Sidney the bear didn't like this at all. Fancy making a fuss of a silly little mouse, and giving him treats like that. He would very much have liked the crumb and the lemonade himself.

He pressed himself in the middle and growled furiously when the mouse had gone.

"Don't have that mouse here again," he said. "I don't like hearing somebody else being called Sidney. Anyway, I don't believe his name *is* Sidney. It's not a name for a mouse."

"Well, for all you know, his name might be Sidney Gordon Eustace just like yours," said Amelia Jane at once.

"Pooh! Whoever heard of a mouse having a grand name like that?" said the bear.

"Well, next time you won't do a job, we'll call all three names down the hole," said Amelia, "and see if the little mouse will answer to them!"

Next night there was going to be a party. Everyone had to help to get ready for it. Amelia Jane called to the little bear.

"Sidney, come and set the tables for the party. Sidney, do you hear me?"

Sidney did, but he pretended not to, of course. He wouldn't set party tables! So he went deaf again, and didn't even turn his head.

"Sidney Gordon Eustace, do as you're told or you won't come to the party," bawled the big teddy bear in a rage.

The little bear didn't answer.

Amelia Jane gave a sudden grin. "Never mind," she said. "We'll get Sidney Gordon Eustace, the little mouse, to come and set the tables. He does them beautifully and never breaks a thing. He can come to the party afterwards. I'll call him."

The little bear turned his head. "He won't answer to *that* name, you know he won't!" he said, scornfully. "Call away! No mouse ever had a name as grand as mine."

Amelia Jane went to the mouse-hole and called down it. "Sidney Gordon Eustace, are you there?" she called. "If you are at home, come up and help us. Sidney Gordon Eustace, are you there?"

And at once there came the pattering of tiny feet and, with a loud squeak, the little mouse peeped out of his hole, his whiskers quivering.

"Ah – you are at home," said Amelia. "Well, dear little Sidney, will you set the tables for us? We're going to have a party!"

The mouse was delighted. He was soon at work, and in a short while the four tables were set with tiny tablecloths and china. Then he went to help the dolls' house dolls to cut sandwiches.

The little bear watched all this out of the corner of his eye. He was quite amazed that the mouse had come when he was called Sidney Gordon Eustace – goodness, fancy a common little mouse owning a name like that!

He was very cross when he saw that the mouse was going to the party. Amelia Jane found him a red ribbon to tie round his neck and one for his long tail. He was given a place at the biggest table, and everyone made a fuss of him.

"Good little Sidney! You do work well! Whatever should we do without you? What will you have to eat?"

The mouse ate a lot. Much too much,

the little bear thought. *He* didn't go to the party. He hadn't been asked and he didn't quite like to go because there was no chair for him and no plate. But, oh, all those nice things to eat! *Why* hadn't he been sensible and gone to set the tables?

"Goodnight, Sidney Gordon Eustace," said Amelia to the delighted mouse. "We've loved having you."

After this kind of thing had happened three or four times the bear got tired of it. He hated hearing people yell for "Sidney, Sidney!" down the mouse-hole or hearing the mouse addressed as Sidney Gordon Eustace. It was really too bad. Also, the mouse was getting all the titbits and the treats. The bear didn't like that either.

So the next time that there was a job to be done, the bear decided to do it. He suddenly heard the rabbit say, "Hello! The big red engine is very smeary. It wants a polish again. I'll go and call Sidney."

The pink rabbit went to the mouse-hole and began to call down it. "Sidney, Sidney, Sidney!"

But before the mouse could answer, Sidney the bear rushed up to the rabbit. "Yes! Did you call me? What do you want me to do?"

"Dear me, you're not as deaf as usual," said the rabbit, surprised. "Well, go and polish the red engine, then. You can have a sweet out of the toy sweet shop if you do it properly."

Sidney did do it properly.

The pink rabbit came and looked at the engine and so did Amelia Jane.

"Very nice," said Amelia. "Give him a big sweet, Rabbit."

The bear was pleased. He had done the mouse out of a job. The toys had been pleased with him, and the sweet was delicious.

And after that, you should have seen Sidney the bear rush up whenever his name was called. "Yes, yes – here I am. What do you want me to do?"

Very soon the little mouse was not called up the hole any more and Sidney the bear worked hard and was friendly and sensible.

The toys began to like him, and Sidney liked them, too.

But one thing puzzled the rabbit and the big teddy bear, and they asked Amelia Jane about it.

"Amelia Jane – how did you know that the mouse's name was Sidney Gordon Eustace?"

"It isn't," said Amelia with a grin.

"But it must be," said the rabbit. "He always came when you called him by it."

"I know – but he'd come if you called *any* name down his hole," said Amelia. "Go and call what name you like – he'll come! It's the calling he answers, not the name. He doesn't even know what names are."

"Good gracious!" said the rabbit and the bear, and they went to the mouse-hole.

"William," called Rabbit, and up came the mouse. He was given a crumb and went down again.

"Polly-Wolly-Doodle," shouted the big bear, and up came the mouse for another crumb.

"Boot-polish," shouted Rabbit, and up came the mouse.

"Tomato soup," cried the big bear.

It didn't matter what name was shouted down the hole, the mouse always came up. He came because he heard a loud shout, that was all.

Amelia Jane went into fits of laughter when the mouse came up at different calls. Penny stamp! Cough-drop! Sid-Sid-Sid! Dickory-Dock! Rub-a-dub-dub!

The mouse's nose appeared at the hole each time. How the toys laughed – all except Sidney the bear!

He didn't laugh. He felt very silly indeed. Oh, dear, what a trick Amelia Jane had played on him. But suddenly he began to laugh, too. "It's funny," he cried. "It's funny!"

In the King's shoes

Once upon a time the brownie pedlar Twiddles was sitting down by the lane-side mending a kettle. As he sat there, who should come along but the King of Brownie Land himself! He was walking slowly, as if he were tired. He saw Twiddles sitting by the lane-side and he sat down by him.

"Your Majesty, can I run to the nearest cottage and get a chair for you?" said Twiddles, jumping up and bowing.

"No," said the King. "Let me sit in the grass for once if I wish to. My shoes hurt me. I shall take them off for a few minutes while I talk to you."

The King slipped off his beautiful,

highly polished shoes with their silver laces.

"My word!" said Twiddles the pedlar. "I'd dearly love to be in your shoes for a little while, Your Majesty."

"You would, would you?" said the King. "Well, it's a silly, foolish wish of yours, but I'll grant it! Get into my shoes – and you'll find yourself King! I'll be a pedlar for a few happy hours!"

Hardly believing his ears, Twiddles got into the King's shoes. They fitted him perfectly. He stood up and gazed down at himself in astonishment. He was dressed like a king – and the King was dressed like a pedlar! Such was the magic in the King's shoes! Whoever wore them could be the King himself!

"Go down the lane and you'll meet my servants," said the King. "Good luck to you! I'm going to have a snooze in the shade here and listen to the birds singing."

Twiddles went down the lane, holding his head high, and looking as proud

as could be. He was King! King! How grand it felt!

He saw some men hurrying towards him.

"Your Majesty, Your Majesty!" they cried. "You will be late for the opening of that sale of work. Hurry, Sire!"

"Dear me," thought Twiddles, "so I am to open a sale of work, and everyone will bow to me and cheer me. How fine!"

He hurried to a waiting carriage and climbed into it. He drove off quickly to the next town. How the people there cheered him! He opened the sale of work, and read a speech that was put before him. He stood in the hot sun for about an hour, shaking hands with all kinds of brownies. He began to feel tired.

"I say, isn't it about time for dinner?" he asked a courtier nearby.

"Not nearly," said the brownie, looking surprised. "You have to review your troops of Scouts next, Your Majesty. Have you forgotten?"

"Oh, well," thought Twiddles, "it will be fun to ask the Scouts all about their camp fires and the best way to boil kettles on them. I am sure I could teach them a thing or two about that!"

But, to his surprise, when he began to talk to the Scouts about this sort of thing his courtiers nudged his arm and frowned.

"Your Majesty is not supposed to know how kettles are boiled or camp fires made!" they whispered. "Those are not the things a king is interested in."

"Dear me!" thought Twiddles. "How dull it must be to be a king all one's life! How hungry I am getting! Whenever are we going to have dinner? I guess it will be a fine one, with lots of marvellous things to eat and drink!"

But, to his great disgust, as soon as he had finished with the Scouts he was hustled into his carriage and driven off to see a new ship being launched – and a footman presented him with a little packet of sandwiches to eat!

"Is this all my dinner?" asked poor Twiddles. "Just sardine sandwiches? Well, well, well! I'd be better off if I were a pedlar! I'd at least fry myself bacon and eggs, with an apple or two to follow!"

"Your Majesty, there is no time for you to have a proper lunch today," said the courtier who was with him. "You have to be at the dockyards in half an hour. And after that you have to visit a hospital. And then there is the flower show to go to."

"Do you mean to say that all these things are on one day?" asked Twiddles in disgust. "Don't I get any time off at all?"

"Your Majesty is acting very strangely today," said the courtier, looking troubled. "You promised to do all these things – and a king must keep his promise."

Twiddles launched the new ship. He rushed off to the hospital, and walked round and round the wards, and spoke to everyone in the beds there. By the time he had finished his feet felt as if they could not walk another step, and his face was stiff with smiling so much. He badly wanted a cup of tea.

But no! He had to go to the flower show next, and miss out his tea altogether! He was still very hungry, as he had only had the sandwiches for dinner.

He yawned and yawned at the flower show, and his courtiers looked most disgusted with him. He didn't at all want to see the beautiful flowers they showed him. He didn't want to smell any of them. He just wanted to sit down on a chair and have a cup of tea all by himself.

When the flower show was over he was driven to the palace.

Twiddles was thrilled to see it shining in the evening sun. The people cheered him as he passed. Twiddles forgot about his dull and tiring day and waved his hat to the people. But that was not the thing to do at all. He had to bow stiffly from left to right and from right to left. He got out of the carriage and went up the long flight of steps.

"I want a jolly good meal now," he said to the courtiers.

They looked surprised. "Your Majesty, you will only just have time to change into your best uniform and get ready for the big military dinner you are giving tonight," they said.

"Oh, well," thought Twiddles, "I shall certainly have something to eat at the dinner – and I shall look very handsome in a uniform, too."

The uniform was tight and stiff. It cut him round the legs. It cut him across the shoulders. It was heavy. But still, he did look very handsome indeed. He went down to the dinner.

But before he could sit down he found that he had to shake hands with two hundred guests! Twiddles was not used to shaking hands with so many people and his hand soon ached terribly. At last he sat down to the table.

He had a famous general on one side, and a famous prince on the other. They both talked so much that Twiddles hardly had time to eat anything, because he had to keep saying, "Yes, certainly," and, "No, of course not!" almost every moment.

The dinner took a long, long time. Twiddles got very bored. He thought the general and the prince were both very silly. He wished they would stop talking for just one minute. But they didn't.

At last bedtime came. Twiddles felt as if he was being squeezed to death in his tight uniform. He could hardly breathe. He was so very, very glad to get out of it. His servants left him when he was ready for bed. He stood and looked at the beautiful bed ready for him – and he shook his head.

"No," said Twiddles. "I don't want to sleep in you – and wake up in the morning to rush about all day long doing things I don't want to do. It's a difficult thing to be a king. I'd rather be a pedlar. I'm free, but a king is not. A king has many masters and must do as he is told all day long – a pedlar has no master and is as free as the air! I'm going back to be a pedlar again!"

He slipped out of the palace in his sleeping-suit. He made his way to the stables. He jumped on a horse, and rode bareback to the lane-side where he had left the King.

There was a small light there – the remains of a camp fire. A man was sleeping peacefully beside it. It was the real King!

Twiddles woke him. "Wake up!" he said. "I've come back. I'm not a good king! I got hungry and bored. I'd rather be a pedlar."

The King sat up and stared at him.

"Well, I got hungry and bored, too, when I was a king," he said. "I like being a pedlar. It's lovely! Just do what you like, and nobody to say, 'It's your duty to do this or that!' No, Twiddles, you go on being a king. I don't want to go back."

Twiddles kicked off the King's shoes. He had put them on to come back in. In a trice he had changed once again to the untidy pedlar he had been that morning. Even his beautiful sleeping-suit disappeared and he was dressed in his same old clothes. But the King was dressed in the fine sleeping-suit – he was no longer a pedlar!

The King got up. "Well, well," he said, "I suppose I had better go back. After all, it's my job. I must do it as well as I can for the sake of my people, who love me. But oh, Pedlar, you can't think how I have enjoyed today!"

"Yes, I can," said Twiddles, patting the King kindly on the back. "You've enjoyed today just as much as *I* shall enjoy tomorrow. Now, goodnight, Your Majesty, and pleasant dreams!"

Twiddles lay down by the fire. The King galloped back to the palace on the horse. And when the pedlar awoke next morning he wasn't at all sure that it was nothing but a dream!

"Poor old King!" he said. "He has the hardest job in the world. Won't I cheer him when I next see him! But I wouldn't be in *his* shoes for anything!"

The goblin and the dragon

O nce upon a time there was a green goblin called Crooky. He was just like his name, as crooked a goblin as ever lived in Little Town. He didn't tell the truth, he took things belonging to other people, and he was the worst tale-teller anyone could imagine.

No one liked him, no one smiled at him and no one asked him out to tea. Crooky hadn't a single friend, and didn't want one. He was only welcomed by witches, because he sometimes captured prisoners for them to make into servants. He was paid well for that, and was very rich.

Up on the hill behind Little Town was a deep cave. In this cave lived Goofle

the dragon. He was quite harmless, but once in a while he would get terribly hungry; then all the pixies and brownies and goblins kept out of his way till he had fed on the cartful of bananas that the Lord High Chamberlain sent him as soon as he knew the dragon was hungry again. It was said that Goofle might forget his liking for bananas and eat a pixie, if one was near at that time.

Crooky often saw the dragon, because the goblin's house was near the cave. But Goofle didn't like Crooky at all, and wouldn't speak to him. He knew that he was a bad goblin and even dragons like to choose their friends.

This made Crooky very cross, and he was always trying to get Goofle to be friendly with him, so that he might be able to say, "The dragon asked me to tea in his cave," or "The dragon had a picnic with me yesterday," as the other little folk did. But Goofle turned his head away and sniffed loudly whenever Crooky came near, and wouldn't have anything to do with him at all.

Now one day Crooky went to a meeting to hear what arrangements were to be made to greet the King when he came on his yearly visit to Little Town. A pixie and an elf began to quarrel, and all the others tried to stop them.

"Be quiet, Flip!" cried the brownies near by. "You look as ugly as the old dragon when you frown like that!"

"Don't lose your temper, Gobo!" cried the pixies to the elf. "You will grow as ugly as the dragon if you do!"

Now as soon as Crooky heard them calling out these things, a plan came into his mind. Suppose he went to tell the dragon that the little folk called him ugly, surely Goofle would be pleased with him, and would be so angry with the other folk that he would go into the town and eat them all up. Then he and Goofle would be friends, and perhaps the dragon would make Crooky King of Little Town.

"Now, that's a good idea of mine," said Crooky to himself, and he slipped out of the meeting-hall to think about it. "I will pretend to be very much grieved to think that anyone should call Goofle ugly, and I will tell him he is beautiful, and that he should punish those who think he is not. He will be my friend after that, and everything will be lovely."

So the very next day Crooky started out to the dragon's cave. Goofle was lying out in the sun, having a sun-bathe. He was not beautiful – indeed he really was very ugly, for he had scales all over his body, a long spiky tail, and when he breathed, smoke came out of his nose.

"Hello, Goofle," said Crooky, in a very cheerful friendly voice. The dragon took no notice of him, and pretended not to see or hear him.

"*Hello, Goofle!*" shouted Crooky. "I say, I've got something to tell you. You *will* be surprised to hear it. It's something I've heard about you, and you won't be a bit pleased to hear what people say about you. As I feel very friendly towards you, I thought it was my duty to tell you."

Goofle said nothing. He yawned very widely, and shut his eyes. Then, quite suddenly he felt terribly hungry. Once every fifty days he felt like that, and it just happened to be the fiftieth day that morning. He wondered whether the Lord High Chamberlain was sending his cartful of bananas, and he opened his eyes to look down the hill to see if it was coming.

But it wasn't. The Lord High Chamberlain had made a mistake for once, and thought that it was only the forty-ninth day. The bananas were ordered for the next day instead.

Crooky the goblin didn't know that it was the fiftieth day. He went quite near to the dragon and spoke to him once more.

"Do listen, Goofle," he said. "I have something surprising to tell you. Do you know that everyone calls you ugly? What do you think of that?"

Goofle put his paw behind his ear, and pretended that he was hard of hearing, though he could quite well hear every word that the horrid little goblin was saying.

"Come nearer," he said. "I'm deaf in one ear and can't hear out of the other. Come nearer, Crooky!"

So Crooky came nearer.

"Sit on the end of my tail, Crooky," said the dragon. "I'm terribly deaf this morning. Sit on my tail."

So the little tell-tale sat on the end of the dragon's spiky tail, and began to speak again.

"People down in Little Town say that you are very ugly," he said. "I think you ought to eat people that say unkind things about you. I think you are very beautiful."

Goofle pretended he still couldn't hear.

"Sit on my back," he said. "There's a buzzing in one of my ears and a singing noise in the other. I can't hear what you say. Sit on my back, Crooky."

So Crooky sat on the dragon's back, and began to shout. But Goofle only shook his head.

"One ear's deaf and the other's no good," he said. "Sit on my head, Crooky, sit on my head."

So Crooky sat on the dragon's head, and began to shout again. But still it didn't seem to make the dragon hear.

"Sit on my big front tooth, Crooky," he said. "Sit on my big front tooth."

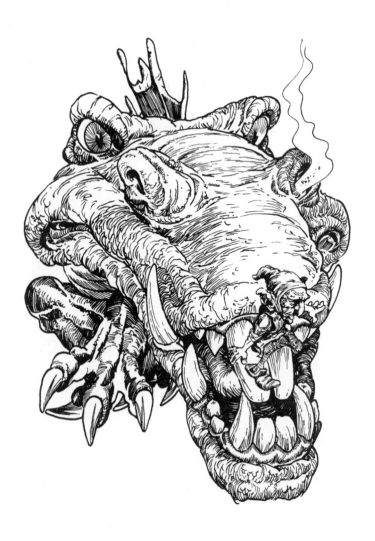

So Crooky sat on the dragon's big front tooth – and then Goofle opened his mouth very wide indeed, jerked back his head, and shut his teeth with a snap.

Where was Crooky? He was gone! The dragon smiled a wide smile, and felt that he could wait for his bananas now. In the distance he saw two or three brownies and he called to them.

"Ho there, brownies!" he cried. "Come here a moment. Crooky said you call me ugly. I hope that that is true. You *do* think I'm ugly, don't you?"

"Of course we do," said the brownies, in surprise. "We have always told you so, Goofle. There isn't such a thing as a beautiful dragon, as you very well know. It is right for you to be ugly."

"I thought so," said Goofle with a pleased sigh. "That stupid Crooky called me beautiful, and it made me feel so angry. I couldn't *bear* to be a beautiful dragon! Why, everyone would laugh at me!"

"Where is Crooky now?" asked the

brownies, looking round. "We will scold him for trying to tell tales. He is the horridest goblin that ever lived!"

The dragon went red, and hung his head.

"Well, you see," he said. "Crooky sat on my big front tooth – and when I opened my mouth, he fell down my throat. I'm afraid you won't see him any more."

"Good gracious!" cried the brownies in a fright. "Why, it must be the fiftieth day! We must go and see about your bananas!"

Off they scurried and sent a message to the Lord High Chamberlain begging him to send the bananas at once. Then they went to tell the news about Crooky to everyone in Little Town.

Nobody said they were sorry, and nobody said they were glad – but Little Town was *ever* so much nicer without Crooky! As for Goofle the dragon, he ate up every one of his bananas, and then went to sleep very happy.

Goldie and the water sprite

G oldie was a fine goldfish. He lived in a big glass globe on the playroom bookcase, and swam about by himself all day long. In the globe was some green water-weed, three water-snails, an empty sea shell, and at the bottom, a few clean, white stones.

Goldie was proud of his home. Everyone who came to the playroom said how pretty it looked, with all the green water-weed floating about the water. The goldfish belonged to Minnie and Beth, the two little girls who lived in the house.

At night he had a lovely time. All the toys used to creep from their shelves and out of the toy cupboard and play games with each other. Goldie used to watch them, and often the dolls would climb up to his shelf and talk to him.

Sometimes they would bring with them a little floating duck, and float it on Goldie's water. The duck loved that, and Goldie was pleased when the little creature dived down into the water and said what a beautiful fish he was.

One day Minnie and Beth, who were twins, had a birthday. Their Auntie Susan gave them a lovely toy. It was a circus, with elephants, horses, clowns, lions and bears. There was a band too, made of little men, each with a trumpet, drum or horn. Minnie and Beth thought the circus was lovely, and they played with it all day long.

When bedtime came they left it out on the floor. As soon as the house was quiet and dark the toys ran up to see what the circus was like. Then all the elephants, horses and clowns came to life!

"We'll give you a fine show!" said one of the clowns to the toys around. "Come along and sit down. Now, band, strike up and play a merry tune!"

The band struck up and soon a lively march was heard in the playroom. The circus began. The elephants performed, the horses danced, the lions and bears did their tricks and the clowns made everyone laugh.

Goldie saw that something was happening, and he pushed his nose against the side of the glass globe and tried to see what it was. He heard the sound of the band and it made him excited.

"Oh, I *wish* I could see what they're doing!" he thought, waving his tail from side to side. "Why doesn't someone come up and tell me? What lovely music! I feel as if I want to go mad with joy when I hear it!"

The band made him feel so frisky that he began to rush all about the water. Then suddenly he gave a great leap upwards, and jumped right out of the glass globe!

Flop! He fell on the floor and all the breath was shaken out of his glittering body. "Ah!" he thought. "Now I shall be able to go and see what all the excitement is about!"

But, alas for Goldie! He found that he couldn't breathe out of the water! He began to gasp, and wriggled about on the floor, wondering why he couldn't swim.

The toys heard the flop and looked round. The circus stopped in a hurry.

"Ooh, it's Goldie!" cried the teddy bear in a fright. "He's jumped out and he can't get back!"

"Whatever shall we do?" said a clown, hurrying up to the struggling fish. "We can't get him back to the water, he's too big and slippery."

"Oh, Goldie, dear Goldie, you'll die out of the water," sobbed one of the dolls.

All the toys stood round the gasping goldfish, wondering what to do. Then the little floating duck had an idea.

"Let's fetch the water sprite who lives

all alone out in the pond," it said. "Perhaps she will know what to do."

So a wooden soldier was sent to fetch the sprite, and she soon came hurrying in, her wet hair hanging down her back. When she saw the poor goldfish on the floor, she was very upset.

"We must get him quickly back to the water," she said, "or else he will die. Where does he live?"

"In the glass globe on the bookcase," said the teddy bear, pointing upwards.

"Goodness!" said the sprite. "We can't get him up there! What in the world shall we do?"

She looked round the playroom, and saw the dolls' house. She ran inside, and in a trice was out again.

"There's a bath in there," she said to the teddy bear. "Fetch it out quickly. Then take some jugs from the dresser in the doll's house kitchen, and fill them with water from the glass globe. Put the water in the bath and fill it as quickly as you can. Then we'll lift the goldfish

into it. He's nearly as big as the bath is, but if he lies still, he will be all right till morning."

All the toys ran to do what she said. The dolls' tin bath was dragged out, and the little jugs were taken from the dresser. Soon they were filled with water, which was poured into the bath.

All this time Goldie lay on the floor. He was so weak and breathless now that he could hardly move. He felt sure he was going to die.

At last the bath was full.

"Now!" cried the sprite. "The teddy, the clown and one of the dolls must lift Goldie up gently and carry him to the bath. Put him into the water, and see if he is all right."

"Oh, poor Goldie, he's dead, I'm sure he's dead!" wept the fairy doll, as she saw the goldfish lying quite still. The teddy bear, the big doll and a clown went to him and lifted him gently in their arms. They carried him to the bath very slowly, for he was heavy.

Then they slipped him into the water.

All the toys crowded round to see if he would come to life. For some time he made no movement at all. Then, very feebly, he moved his tail and opened his mouth to take in water.

"He's alive, he's alive!" cried the toys in delight. "We've saved him!"

In half an hour's time Goldie was quite all right again, and wasn't he astonished to find himself in the dolls' bath! The teddy bear explained to him what had happened, and he was very grateful.

"I'll lie here quite still till the morning," he said. "Then I expect Minnie and Beth will find me, and put me back into my glass globe again. It's really very kind of you all to have saved me."

"It was the water sprite that really saved your life," said the teddy. "It was her idea to put you into the bath. We should never have thought of it."

Next morning Minnie and Beth found

Goldie lying in their dolls' bath. They *were* astonished!

"Oh, look, Mummy!" they cried. "Goldie's got out of his globe to have a bath! Isn't he funny! Let's put him back again. However did he get there?"

But Mummy couldn't answer *that* question. She was just as puzzled as the twins.

That isn't quite all the story. When the water sprite came to ask about Goldie the next day, she slid down into the fish's globe and swam up to him.

"Ooh!" she said, with delight. "Your water feels so nice and warm after the cold pond outside, Goldie! It's so lonely there too – there isn't a single fish I can talk to."

"Well," said Goldie, "I'm rather lonely here myself – wouldn't you like to come and share my home with me? You could live in that empty sea shell at the bottom."

"Oh, I'd *love* to!" cried the sprite, and

she straightaway crept into the shell and cuddled there. And now Goldie and the sprite live together as happy as can be. If you want to see her in the daytime, you'll know where to look – in the sea shell that lies at the bottom of Goldie's globe!

Oh, what a pity!

Tessie had a bicycle, and all the other boys and girls thought she was very lucky, because it really was a nice one.

At first she lent it to anyone who wanted to try and ride it, but when Harry had dented the mudguard, and Jane had broken a pedal, Tessie's mother said she was not to lend it to any child except in her own garden.

Susan was cross when she heard this. "Oh, how mean of your mother!" she said. "She might let you lend it in the road, Tessie!"

"Mummy isn't mean," said Tessie, who would never let anyone say a word against her mother. "It's just that she paid a lot of money for my bike, and she doesn't want it spoilt. She's not mean."

"Well, you ask me to tea and then I can ride your bike in the garden," said Susan. So Tessie told her mother that Susan wanted to come to tea so that she could ride the bicycle.

"Susan always wants to push in and get her own way," said Tessie's mother. "No, I can't have her to tea just yet, Tessie. You are having your cousin for the day this week, and Harry is coming to tea on Tuesday. You can't have Susan."

Susan was cross. "Well, I said it before and I say it again – your mother is mean!" she said to Tessie. Tessie walked off without a word. She was not going to quarrel with Susan, but she wasn't going to stay with her if she said things like that.

Susan soon tried to make Tessie friends with her again, because she so badly wanted to ride Tessie's bicycle. So she gave her a sweet, and told her that she was the nicest girl in the class.

When Tessie was sucking the sweet and was nice and friendly once more, Susan asked for a ride.

"Let me have a little ride, just a tiny little ride on your bike," she said. "We'll wait till all the other boys and girls have gone, Tessie, then no one will see. I'll ride it down the lane, that's all. Please do let me."

"Mummy said I wasn't to," said Tessie.

"Well," said Susan, thinking of another idea. "Well, Tessie, you just turn your back for a minute – and I'll hop on the bike and ride off without you seeing. Then it won't matter, because, you see, you won't have *lent* me the bike, I shall have taken it. Please, please, do let me have a ride, Tessie. You're so lucky to have a bike."

"Well," said Tessie, hardly liking to say no, because she saw how much Susan wanted a ride. "Well – just this once, then."

She turned her back. Susan jumped

on to the bike and rode away down the lane. How fast she rode! How grand she felt!

Just as she passed a field-gate a cow came out, the first of a herd driven out by the farmer. Susan was so frightened that she wobbled, and fell off. Crash! She fell on her side and grazed her arm badly, and tore her dress.

Tessie heard the crash and turned. She ran to Susan and helped her up. "Oh – I knew I shouldn't have let you ride my bike," she said. "I knew I shouldn't! Look at your poor arm – and what will your mother say to your torn dress?"

The bicycle was not hurt, which was lucky. Susan picked it up, brushed her frock down, and looked at her bleeding arm. "Bother!" she said. "That tiresome cow! It made me fall off."

"Well, you shouldn't have been on the bike, should you, really?" said Tessie, taking it. "You shouldn't have told me to turn my head away so that you could take it without my seeing you. It's a good thing the bike isn't damaged. Mummy *would* have been cross with you – and with me, too, for disobeying her."

Susan went home, trying to hide her torn dress and grazed arm. But her mother saw them both at once.

"Susan! What have you done to your arm? Did you fall down? And how did you tear your dress?"

"I was riding Tessie's bike," said Susan, not liking to tell her mother a story. "A cow came out of a gate and scared me, and I fell off."

"Susan, you are *not* to ride other people's bicycles," said her mother, at once. "For two reasons – one is that you may damage someone else's bike, and the other is that you haven't had enough practice in riding, and until you have you are not to ride in the road. You might have a bad accident."

"I shouldn't," said Susan, looking sulky.

"Now, do you understand, Susan?" said her mother. "I mean it. You are *not* to ride Tessie's bicycle, or anyone else's. One day you shall have one of your own, and then you can practise riding it round and round your own garden till you can ride well enough to go out into the road. Be patient and wait till then."

Susan didn't feel at all patient. How could she wait perhaps for years for a bicycle? She knew that a bicycle was expensive, and she knew that her mother hadn't a lot of money to spare. She might have to wait till she was twelve before she had a bicycle — and she wasn't even nine till next week! How she wished she could have a bicycle for her ninth birthday! That would be grand.

Her arm soon healed. Her dress was mended. Once or twice her mother warned her to remember what she had said about Tessie's bicycle.

"You will remember that I don't want you to ride Tessie's bicycle again, won't you?" she said. "And I hear that Tessie's mother has asked her not to lend it to anyone, too – so on no account must you borrow it, Susan."

Susan didn't say anything. She meant to have another ride whenever she could! Her mother noticed that she said nothing and spoke sharply.

"Susan! Will you promise me not to ride on Tessie's bicycle?" she said.

"All right," said Susan, sulkily. How tiresome to have to promise! "I wish I could have a bike for my birthday next week, Mummy! Tessie was only nine when she had hers."

"Bicycles are so expensive," said Susan's mother. "And you are not very old yet. There is plenty of time for you to have a bicycle, Susan!"

Susan didn't ask Tessie for a ride any more that week. She watched her riding to and from school very enviously, but she didn't beg for a turn, too. She didn't want to upset Tessie, or to break her own promise.

The next week came. The day before her birthday came, Susan told everyone it was her birthday the next day, and she felt excited because she knew her mother was making her a cake with nine candles on it, and she thought she was having a work-basket and a new book, too.

Now, as Susan went home from school that afternoon, she suddenly saw Tessie's bicycle leaning against the wall that ran round Harry's garden in the main road! Yes, there it was, bright and shining. Tessie must have gone in to see Harry's white mice.

"The road's empty. I'll just jump on Tessie's bike and have a little ride!" thought Susan. "No one will know. I'll go round the corner and back."

Quite forgetting her promise, Susan jumped on the bicycle and rode down the road. She went fast, pedalling up and down strongly. She rang her bell at the corner. Ting-a-ling-a-ling! It sounded fine.

Then she put the brakes on to see if they worked. But they didn't work very well. Tessie had been told that she must take her bicycle to the shop to have the brakes put right, or else she might have an accident.

"Now I'd better go back," thought Susan to herself, and turned to go back. She had pedalled up the hill, and now it would be fun to go down it without pedalling at all!

She simply *flew* down! It was quite a steep hill. Suddenly, round the corner, came the big old cart-horse belonging to the farmer, dragging a heavy cart behind him.

Susan wobbled. She rang her bell but the horse took no notice. She put on the brakes to slow the bicycle down – but they didn't work! The bicycle flew on and on, and it seemed as if the big horse and cart blocked up the whole of the road.

Just as she reached the horse, Susan tried to jump off the bike. But it was going too fast for her to jump properly. She slipped, the bicycle flew straight into the alarmed horse, and Susan herself rolled over and over and over towards the side of the road.

She sat up, gasping, looking at herself to see if she was hurt. But she wasn't! There didn't seem even to be a bruise or a scratch.

Then she looked round for the bicycle. But oh, what a pity, it was completely spoilt! The frightened horse had reared up when Susan had run into it, and had brought its heavy, enormous hoofs down on to the bicycle. The wheels were buckled and broken. The handle was twisted. The right pedal was off and the left one was bent.

"Oh! Look at Tessie's bike!" said Susan, with tears in her eyes. The farmer was trying to pull it from his horse's feet. He thought the bicycle was Susan's.

"I'm afraid your bike's done for," he said. "Why did you ride so fast down

the hill? That was silly of you. You frightened my horse terribly. He might have run away."

Susan didn't know what to do. Crying bitterly, she dragged the poor, broken bike home at last, and her mother came running out to see whatever was the matter.

"Oh, Mummy – oh, Mummy – look at Tessie's bike!" wept Susan. "I broke my promise. I took it when Tessie was at Harry's – and I ran into a horse, and the horse stamped on the bike. Oh, Mummy, what shall I do?"

Her mother looked in horror at the bicycle. "Are you hurt?" she said to Susan. Susan shook her head. "Well, you might easily have been killed, Susan. And *look* at Tessie's bike! Whatever will her father and mother say?"

"I don't know, I don't know!" wailed Susan. "Oh, why did I disobey you and break my promise? Tell me what I'm to do!"

Susan's mother looked very grave. She set the broken bicycle by the fence, and took Susan's arm. "Come with me," she said. "I will show you what you must do."

She took Susan to a shed, which was locked. She unlocked it. Inside was a brand-new, very beautiful, shining bicycle! Susan gave a gasp when she saw it.

"Look," said her mother. "Daddy and I bought this for your birthday tomorrow, for a big surprise. Now, Susan, I am afraid you must take it to Tessie instead, because you have completely spoilt *her* bicycle. Maybe we can get Tessie's mended up for you – I don't know – but you will certainly have to give up your new bicycle to Tessie."

Oh, what a pity! Oh, what a terrible pity to have to give up such a beautiful bicycle to somebody else, all because of a moment's disobedience and a broken promise. How Susan cried! How she wept and wailed! But she knew her mother was right. It was the only thing to do.

So now Tessie has Susan's beautiful bicycle, and Susan is waiting to hear if Tessie's old one can be mended. Poor Susan – it was very hard for her, wasn't it, but, as her mother said, you never know *what* may happen if you are disobedient, or break a solemn promise!